WANTED

Wanted

A PRETTY LITTLE LIARS NOVEL

SARA SHEPARD

HARPER TEEN
An Imprint of HarperCollinsPublishers

alloy**entertainment**
Produced by Alloy Entertainment
151 West 26th Street, New York, NY 10001

Library of Congress Cataloging-in-Publication Data is available.

ISBN 978-0-06-156617-2

Design by Elizabeth Dresner

10 11 12 13 14   CG/RRDB   10 9 8 7

First Edition

To three English teachers:
The late Mary French, Alice Campbell, and Karen Bald Mapes.

*There are two tragedies in life. One is to lose your heart's desire.
The other is to gain it.*

—GEORGE BERNARD SHAW

LOOK AGAIN

They say a picture's worth a thousand words. A surveillance camera catches a beautiful brunette making off with a handful of gold Tiffany baubles. A paparazzi shot exposes an affair between a young starlet and a married director. But what the picture can't tell you is that the girl was a store clerk taking those bracelets to her boss, or that the director filed for divorce last month.

So what about a family photo? Take, for instance, a shot of a mom, dad, sister, and brother grinning on the front porch of a luxe Victorian mansion. Now look closer. Dad's smile seems kind of forced. Mom's gazing toward the left at a neighbor's house—or maybe at a *neighbor*. Brother grips the porch rail tight, like he wants to crack it in half. And sister smiles mysteriously, as if she's hiding a delicious secret. Half of the backyard is torn up by a giant yellow bulldozer, and there's someone lurking way in the background, nothing but a blur of blond hair and pale skin. Is that a guy . . . or a girl? It could be a trick of the light or a finger smudge.

Or perhaps all those things you missed upon first glance mean much more than you could ever guess.

Four pretty girls in Rosewood believe they have a clear picture of what happened the night their best friend went missing. Someone has been arrested, and the case has been closed. But if they comb through their memories once more, focusing on the flickers in the periphery, the uneasy feelings they can't pin down, and *the people right under their noses*, that picture might change right before their eyes. If they take a deep breath and look again, they might be astonished—even terrified—by what they discover.

Truth is stranger than fiction, after all. Especially here in Rosewood.

The June evening was misty and moonless. Crickets chirped in the thick, black woods, and the whole neighborhood smelled like fresh azaleas, citronella candles, and bleachy pool chlorine. Brand-new luxury cars were tucked away in three-car garages. As with everything else in Rosewood, Pennsylvania, a chic, rustic suburb about twenty miles from Philadelphia, not a blade of grass was out of place, and everyone was exactly where they were supposed to be.

Almost everyone.

Alison DiLaurentis, Spencer Hastings, Aria Montgomery, Emily Fields, and Hanna Marin turned on all the lights in the converted barn apartment behind Spencer's house, settling in for their end-of-seventh-grade sleepover. Spencer quickly dumped several empty Corona bottles into the recycling bin. They'd belonged to her sister, Melissa, and Melissa's boyfriend, Ian Thomas, whom Spencer had banished from the barn moments before. Emily and Aria flung their yellow and maroon LeSportsac overnight totes in a pile in the corner. Hanna flopped on the couch and started munching on leftover popcorn. Ali latched the barn door and turned the dead bolt. No one heard the squish of footsteps in the dewy grass or saw the light fog of breath on the window.

Snap.

"So, girls," Alison piped up, perching on the arm of the leather couch. "I know the perfect thing to do." The window wasn't open, but the glass was thin, and her words carried through the pane, rustling through the calm June night. "I learned how to hypnotize people. I could do you all at once."

There was a long pause. Spencer picked at the waistband of her field hockey skirt. Aria and Hanna exchanged a worried look.

"*Pleeeeze?*" Ali said, pressing her palms together as if in prayer. She glanced over at Emily. "You'll let me hypnotize *you*, right?"

"Um . . ." Emily's voice quavered. "Well . . ."

"I'll do it," Hanna butted in.

Snap.

Whir.

Everyone else reluctantly agreed. How could they not? Ali was the most popular girl at Rosewood Day, the school they attended. Guys wanted to date her, girls wanted to be her, parents thought she was perfect, and she always got everything she wanted. It was a dream come true that Ali had chosen Spencer, Aria, Emily, and Hanna to be part of her clique at the Rosewood Day Charity Drive the year before, transforming each of them from blah, nondescript Nobodies to important, sparkling Somebodies. Ali took them on weekend trips to the Poconos, gave them mud masks, and provided the golden ticket to the best table in the cafeteria. But she also forced them to do things they didn't want to do—like The Jenna Thing, a horrific secret they vowed to keep until they died. Sometimes they felt like lifeless dolls, with Ali coordinating their every move.

Lately, Ali had been ignoring their calls, hanging out with her older field hockey friends, and was seemingly only interested in the girls' secrets and shortcomings. She teased Aria about her dad's clandestine relationship with one of his students. She poked fun at Hanna's growing obsession with Cheez-Its—and her growing waistline. She mocked Emily's puppy dog crush on her, and threatened to reveal that Spencer had kissed her sister's boyfriend. Each girl suspected their friendship with Ali was slipping through their fingers. Deep down, they wondered if they'd be friends with Ali after tonight.

Snap.

Ali rushed around, lighting the vanilla-scented candles

with a Zippo and pulling the blinds closed—just in case. She told the girls to sit cross-legged on the circular braided rug. They did so, looking fretful and uncomfortable. What might happen if Ali actually managed to hypnotize them? They were all hiding huge secrets that only Ali knew. Secrets they didn't want broadcast to each other, let alone the rest of the world.

Snap.

Whir.

Ali began to slowly count backward from one hundred, her voice feathery and soothing. No one moved. Ali tiptoed around the room, passing the huge oak computer desk, the overstuffed bookshelves, and the tiny kitchen. Everyone remained compliant and statue-still. Never once did anyone look toward the window. Nor did any of them hear the mechanical *snap*s of the clunky old Polaroid camera as it captured their blurry images or the *whir*s as the camera spit out the photos to the ground. There was enough space through one of the slats in the blinds to get a decent picture of all of them.

Snap.

Whir.

When Ali was almost to one, Spencer jumped up and ran right to the back window. "It's too dark in here," Spencer proclaimed. She whipped back the curtains, letting in the night. "I want it lighter. Maybe everyone does."

Alison looked at the others. Their eyes were sealed

closed. Her lips curled up in a smirk. "Close them," she insisted.

Spencer rolled her eyes. "God, take a pill."

Ali glanced out the now-open window. Fear flickered across her face. Did she see? Did she know who was there? Did she know what was coming?

But then Ali turned back to Spencer. Her fingers were curled into fists. "You think *I* should take a pill?"

Snap. Another photo fell from the camera. The image slowly materialized from nothingness.

Spencer and Ali stared at each other for a long time. The other girls remained on the carpet. Hanna and Emily swayed back and forth, tangled in a dream, but Aria's eyes were half open. Her gaze was on Spencer and Ali, watching the fight unfold but feeling powerless to stop it.

"Leave," Spencer demanded, pointing to the door.

"Fine." Ali strode onto the porch, slamming the door hard behind her.

Ali stood for a moment, heaving deep breaths. The leaves on the trees swished and whispered. The yellow lantern-style light over the front door illuminated the left half of Ali's body. There was an angry and determined scowl on her face. She didn't glance fearfully around the side of the house. She didn't sense the dangerous presence that lurked so close. Maybe it was because Ali was preoccupied, keeping a dangerous secret of her own. She had someone to meet right now. And someone else to avoid.

After a moment, Ali started down the path. Seconds later, the barn door slammed again. Spencer followed, catching up with her on the other side of the trees. Their whispers grew more and more fevered and furious. *You try to steal everything away from me. But you can't have this. You read about it in my diary, didn't you? You think kissing Ian was so special, but he told me that you didn't even know how.*

There was the slick, wet sound of shoes slipping on grass. A shriek. A dangerous *crack.* A horrified gasp. And then silence.

Aria stepped out on the porch and looked around. "Ali?" she cried, her bottom lip trembling.

No answer. The tips of Aria's fingers shook; maybe she sensed, deep down, that she wasn't alone.

"Spencer?" Aria called again. She reached out and touched the wind chimes, desperate for sound. They knocked together melodically.

Aria returned to the barn as Hanna and Emily came to. "I had the weirdest dream," Emily murmured, rubbing her eyes. "Ali fell down this really deep well, and there were these giant plants."

"That was my dream, too!" Hanna cried. They stared at each other in confusion.

Spencer stomped back onto the porch, dazed and disoriented.

"Where's Ali?" the other girls asked.

"I don't know," Spencer said in a faraway voice. She looked around. "I thought . . . I don't know."

By this time, the Polaroids had been scooped up off the ground and stowed safely in a pocket. But then the camera went off again by accident, the flash lighting up the red wood siding. Another photo emerged.

Snap. Whir.

The girls stared at the window, frozen and terrified as deer. Was someone there? Ali? Or maybe it was Melissa or Ian. They'd just been here, after all.

They remained very still. Two seconds passed. Five. Ten. There was only silence. It was just the wind, they decided. Or maybe a tree branch scraping against the glass, as painful as someone scraping her fingernails against a plate.

"I think I want to go home," Emily told her friends.

The girls filed out of the barn together—annoyed, embarrassed, shaken. Ali had ditched them. The friendship was over. They started across Spencer's yard, unaware of the terrible things that were to come. The face at the window had disappeared, too, off to follow Ali down the path. Everything had been set in motion. What was about to happen had already begun.

Within hours, Ali would be dead.

1

A BROKEN HOME

Spencer Hastings rubbed her sleep-crusted eyes and put a Kashi waffle in the toaster. Her family's kitchen smelled of freshly brewed coffee, pastries, and lemon-scented household cleaner. The two labradoodles, Rufus and Beatrice, circled her legs, their tails wagging.

The tiny LCD TV in the corner was tuned to the news. A female reporter in a blue Burberry barn jacket was standing with the Rosewood chief of police and a gray-haired man in a black suit. The caption said *The Rosewood Murders*.

"My client has been wrongfully accused," the man in the suit proclaimed. He was William "Billy" Ford's publicly appointed lawyer and it was the first time he'd spoken to the press since Billy's arrest. "He's absolutely innocent. He was framed."

"Right," Spencer spat. Her hand shook unsteadily as she poured coffee into a blue Rosewood Day Prep mug. There was no doubt in Spencer's mind that Billy had killed her best friend, Alison DiLaurentis, nearly four years ago. And now he'd murdered Jenna Cavanaugh, a blind girl in Spencer's grade, and probably Ian Thomas—Melissa's ex-boyfriend, Ali's secret crush, *and* her first accused killer. Cops found a bloody T-shirt that belonged to Ian in Billy's car and they were now searching for his body, though they hadn't come up with any leads.

Outside, a garbage truck grumbled around the cul-de-sac where Spencer lived. A split second later, the same exact sound growled through the speakers of the TV. Spencer walked to the living room and parted the curtains at the front window. Sure enough, a news van was parked at the curb. A cameraman swiveled from one person to the other, and another guy holding a giant microphone braced against the blustery wind. Spencer could see the reporter's mouth moving through the window and hear her voice through the TV speaker.

Across the street, the Cavanaughs' backyard was wrapped in yellow police tape. A cop car had been parked in their driveway ever since Jenna's murder. Jenna's guide dog, a burly German shepherd, peered out the bay window in the living room. He'd remained there day and night for the past two weeks, as if patiently waiting for Jenna to return.

The police had found Jenna's limp, lifeless body in a ditch behind her house. According to reports, Jenna's parents arrived home on Saturday evening to an empty house. Mr. and Mrs. Cavanaugh heard frantic and persistent barks from the back of their property. Jenna's guide dog was tied to a tree . . . but Jenna was gone. When they released the dog, he sprinted straight to the hole plumbers had dug a few days ago to repair a burst water pipe. But there was more inside that hole than the newly fitted pipe. It was as if the murderer *wanted* Jenna to be found.

An anonymous tip led the police to Billy Ford. The cops also charged him with killing Alison DiLaurentis. It made sense—Billy had been a part of the construction crew installing a gazebo for the DiLaurentises the same weekend Ali disappeared. Ali had complained about the lascivious looks the workers gave her. At the time, Spencer had thought Ali was bragging. Now she knew what actually happened. The toaster popped and Spencer padded back to the kitchen. The news had cut back to the studio, where a brunette anchor wearing big hoop earrings sat at a long desk. "Police recovered a series of incriminating images on Mr. Ford's laptop that helped lead to his arrest," the anchor said in a grave voice. "These photos show how closely Mr. Ford was stalking Ms. DiLaurentis, Ms. Cavanaugh, and four other girls known as the Pretty Little Liars."

A montage of old photos of Jenna and Ali appeared, many of the shots looking like they'd been stealthily snapped from a hiding spot behind a tree or inside a car. Then came images of Spencer, Aria, Emily, and Hanna. Some of the pictures were from seventh grade, when Ali was still alive, but others were more recent—there was one of the four girls in dark dresses and heels at Ian's trial, waiting for Ian to show up. There was another shot of them gathered by the Rosewood Day swings clad in wool coats, hats, and mittens, probably discussing New A. Spencer winced.

"There are also messages on Mr. Ford's computer that match the threatening notes sent to Alison's former best friends," the reporter went on. An image of Darren Wilden coming out of a confessional and a bunch of familiar e-mails and IM conversations whizzed past. Each note was signed with a crisp, singular letter *A*. Spencer and her friends hadn't gotten a single message since Billy had been arrested.

Spencer took a gulp of coffee, barely noticing the hot liquid sliding down her throat. It was so bizarre that Billy Ford—a man she didn't know at all—was behind everything that had happened. Spencer had no idea *why* he'd done those things.

"Mr. Ford has a long history of violence," the reporter went on. Spencer peered over her coffee mug. A YouTube video showed a fuzzy image of Billy and a guy in a Phillies cap fighting in a Wawa parking lot. Even after the guy fell to the ground, Billy kept on kicking him. Spencer put her hand to her mouth, picturing Billy doing the same thing to Ali.

"And these images, found in Mr. Ford's car, have never been seen before."

A blurry Polaroid photo materialized. Spencer leaned forward, her eyes widening. It was a shot of the inside of a barn—her *family's* barn, which had been ruined in the fire Billy set several weeks ago, presumably to destroy evidence tying him to Ali's and Ian's murders. In the picture, four girls sat on the round rug in the center of the room, their heads bowed. A fifth girl stood above them, her arms in the air. The next photo was of the same scene, except the standing girl had moved a few inches to the left. In the following shot, one of the girls who had been sitting had stood up and moved toward the window. Spencer recognized the girl's dirty blond hair and rolled-up field hockey skirt. She gasped. She was looking at her younger self. These photos were from the night Ali went missing. Billy had been standing outside the barn, watching them.

And they'd never known.

Someone let out a small, dry cough behind her. Spencer whirled around. Mrs. Hastings sat at the kitchen table, staring blankly into a mug of Earl Grey tea. She was wearing a pair of gray Lululemon yoga pants with a tiny hole in the knee, dirty white socks, and an oversize Ralph Lauren polo. Her hair was stringy, and there were toast crumbs on her left cheek. Normally, Spencer's mom didn't even let the family dogs see her unless she looked absolutely pristine.

"Mom?" Spencer said tentatively, wondering if her mother had seen the Polaroids, too. Mrs. Hastings turned her head slowly, as though she were moving underwater. "Hi, Spence," she said tonelessly. Then she turned back to her tea, staring miserably at the bag steeping at the bottom of the cup.

Spencer bit off the tip of her French-manicured pinkie. On top of everything else, her mom was acting like a zombie . . . and it was all her fault. If only she hadn't blurted out the horrible secret Billy-as-A had told her about her family: that her dad had had an affair with Ali's mother, and that Ali was Spencer's half sister. If only Billy hadn't convinced Spencer that her mom knew about the affair and killed Ali to punish her husband. Spencer had confronted her mother, only to discover that her mother hadn't known—or done—anything. After that, Mrs. Hastings kicked Spencer's dad out of the house, and then more or less gave up on life entirely.

The familiar *click-click-click* of heels on the mahogany hall floors rang through the air. Spencer's sister, Melissa, blustered into the room, surrounded by a cloud of Miss Dior. She wore a pale blue Kate Spade sweater dress and gray kitten heels, and her dark blond hair was pulled back in a gray headband. There was a silver clipboard under her arm and a Montblanc pen behind her right ear.

"Hey, Mom!" Melissa called brightly, giving her a kiss on the forehead. Then she appraised Spencer, setting her mouth in a straight line. "Hey, Spence," she said coolly.

Spencer slumped into the nearest chair. The benevolent, I'm-glad-you're-alive feelings she and her sister had shared the night Jenna was murdered had lasted exactly twenty-four hours. Now, things were back to status quo, with Melissa blaming Spencer for their family's ruin, snubbing

Spencer every chance she got, and taking on all the home responsibilities like the prissy brownnoser she'd always been.

Melissa lifted the clipboard. "I'm going to Fresh Fields for groceries. Want anything special?" She spoke to Mrs. Hastings in an overly loud voice, as if she were ninety years old and deaf.

"Oh, I don't know," Mrs. Hastings said morosely. She stared into her open palms as if they contained great wisdom. "It doesn't really matter, does it? We eat the food, and then it's gone, and then we're hungry again." At that, she stood up, sighed loudly, and shuffled up the stairs to her bedroom.

Melissa's lip twitched. The clipboard knocked against her hip. She glanced over at Spencer, her eyes narrowing. *Look what you've done,* her expression screamed.

Spencer stared out the long line of windows that faced the backyard. Sheets of pale blue ice glistened on the back walkway. Pointed icicles hung from the singed trees. The family's old barn was a heap of black wood and ash, ruined from the fire. The windmill was still in pieces, the word *LIAR* scrawled on the base.

Tears rushed to Spencer's eyes. Whenever she looked at her backyard, she had to resist the urge to run upstairs, curl up under her bed, and shut the door. Things had been great between Spencer and her parents before she exposed the affair—for once. But Spencer now felt the same way she did when she first tasted homemade cappuccino ice cream from the Creamery in Hollis—after just one lick, she had to eat the whole cone. After a taste of what a decent, loving family was like, she couldn't go back to dysfunction and neglect.

The television continued to blare, a picture of Ali filling the screen. Melissa paused to listen for a moment as the reporter walked through the timeline of the murder.

Spencer bit down on her lip. She and Melissa hadn't discussed the fact that Ali was their half sister. Now that Spencer knew that she and Ali were related, it changed everything. For a long time, Spencer had kind of hated Ali—she'd controlled her every move, stockpiled her every secret. But none of that mattered now. Spencer just wished she could go back in time to save Ali from Billy that horrible night.

The station cut to a studio shot of pundits sitting around a high, bistro-style table, discussing Billy's fate. "You can't trust anyone anymore," exclaimed an olive-skinned woman in a cherry-red power suit. "No child is safe."

"Now, wait a second." A black man with a goatee waved his hands to stop them. "Maybe we should give Mr. Ford a chance. A man is innocent until proven guilty, right?"

Melissa scooped up her black patent leather Gucci hobo bag from the island. "I don't know why they're wasting their time discussing this," she spat acidly. "He deserves to rot in hell."

Spencer gave her sister an uneasy look. That was another

strange development in the Hastings household—Melissa had become unequivocally, almost fanatically confident that Billy was the murderer. Every time the news brought up an inconsistency in the case, Melissa grew enraged.

"He'll go to jail," Spencer said reassuringly. "Everyone knows he did it."

"Good." Melissa turned away, plucked the Mercedes car keys out of the ceramic bowl by the phone, buttoned the checkered Marc Jacobs jacket she'd bought at Saks the week before—apparently she wasn't too distraught over their broken home to shop—and slammed the door.

As the pundits continued to squabble, Spencer walked to the front window and watched as her sister backed out of the driveway. There was a disquieting smile on Melissa's lips that sent a shiver up Spencer's backbone.

For some reason, Melissa almost looked . . . *relieved*.

2

THE SECRETS NOW BURIED

Aria Montgomery and her boyfriend, Noel Kahn, huddled close as they walked from the Rosewood Day student parking lot to the lobby entrance. A rush of warm air greeted them as they swept inside the school, but when Aria noticed the display near the auditorium, her blood froze. On a long table across the room was a large photo of Jenna Cavanaugh.

Jenna's porcelain skin shone. Her naturally red lips revealed a hint of a smile. She wore big wraparound Gucci sunglasses that concealed her damaged eyes. *We'll miss you, Jenna*, said gold foil letters above the image. Next to it were smaller pictures, flowers, and other memorabilia and gifts. Someone had added a package of Marlboro Ultra Light cigarettes to the memorial, even though Jenna wasn't the kind of girl who would smoke.

Aria let out a small groan. She'd heard that the school might erect a shrine in Jenna's honor, but something about it seemed so . . . *tacky*.

"Shit," Noel whispered. "We shouldn't have come in this door."

Aria's eyes filled with tears. One minute, Jenna was alive—Aria had seen her at a party at Noel's house, laughing with Maya St. Germain. Then, practically the next minute . . . well, what happened next was too horrible to think about. Aria knew she should be relieved that at least Jenna's killer had been caught, Ali's murder had been solved, and the threatening notes from A had stopped, but what had happened couldn't be undone—an innocent girl was still dead.

Aria couldn't help but wonder if she and her friends could have done more to prevent Jenna's death. When Billy-as-A had been communicating with them, he'd sent Emily a photo of Jenna and Ali when they were younger. He'd then directed Emily to Jenna's house when Jenna and Jason DiLaurentis were fighting. He was obviously giving them a hint about his next victim. Jenna had also recently lingered on Aria's front lawn, looking as though she needed to tell Aria something. When Aria called out to her, Jenna had paled and quickly walked away. Did she sense Billy was going to hurt her? Should Aria have known something was wrong?

A sophomore girl placed a single red rose on the memorial. Aria closed her eyes. She didn't need any more reminders of all that Billy had done. Just that morning she'd seen a report about a set of Polaroids he'd taken of their end-of-seventh-grade sleepover. It was hard to believe

Billy had been so close. As she'd chewed on her quinoa breakfast flakes, she'd parsed her memory of that night over and over, trying to recall anything more. Had she heard any strange noises on the porch or suspicious breathing at the window? Had she felt angry eyes glaring at her through the glass? But she couldn't remember a thing.

Aria leaned against the wall at the far end of the lobby. A bunch of boys on the crew team were crowded around an iPhone, laughing about an app that made a toilet-flushing noise. Sean Ackard and Kirsten Cullen were comparing answers to that day's trig assignment. Jennifer Thatcher and Jennings Silver were making out near the Jenna shrine. Jennifer's hip bumped against the table, knocking over a small photo of Jenna in a shiny gold frame.

A knot tightened in Aria's chest. She marched across the room and straightened the picture. Jennifer and Jennings broke apart, looking guilty.

"Have some respect," Aria snapped at them anyway.

Noel touched Aria's arm. "Come on," he said gently. "Let's get out of here."

He pulled her out of the lobby and around the corner. Kids were at their lockers, hanging up their coats and pulling out books. In a far corner, Shark Tones, Rosewood Day's a cappella group, was rehearsing a version of "I Heard It Through The Grapevine" for an upcoming concert. Aria's brother, Mike, and Mason Byers were in a shoving match near the water fountains.

Aria approached her locker and spun the dial. "It's

like no one even remembers what happened," she murmured.

"Maybe it's their way of dealing," Noel suggested. He rested his arm on Aria's. "Let's do something to get your mind off this."

Aria wriggled out of the houndstooth coat that she'd bought at a thrift store in Philly and hung it on a hook in her locker. "What do you have in mind?"

"Anything you want."

Aria gave him a grateful hug. Noel smelled like spearmint gum and the licorice-scented tree that hung from the rearview mirror of his Cadillac Escalade.

"I wouldn't mind going to Clio tonight," Aria suggested. Clio was a new, quaint café that had opened in downtown Rosewood. The hot chocolates were served in mugs the size of a baseball hat.

"Done," Noel answered. But then he winced and squeezed his eyes shut. "Wait. I can't tonight. I have my support group."

Aria nodded. Noel had lost an older brother to suicide and now attended grief support meetings. After Aria and her old friends had seen Ali's spirit the night Spencer's woods burned down, Aria contacted a medium who told her that *Ali killed Ali*, leading Aria to briefly wonder if Ali had committed suicide, too. "Is it helping?" she asked.

"I think so. Wait—" Noel snapped his fingers at something across the hall. "Why don't we go to that?"

He was pointing to a hot-pink poster. It had black

silhouettes of dancing kids all over it, like the once-ubiquitous iPod ads. But instead of holding Nanos and Touches, they were holding small white hearts. FIND LOVE AT THE VALENTINE'S DAY DANCE THIS SATURDAY, the poster proclaimed in sparkly red letters.

"What do you say?" There was a sweetly vulnerable look on Noel's face. "Want to go with me?"

"Oh!" Aria blurted. Truthfully, she'd wanted to go to the Valentine's Day dance ever since Teagan Scott, a cute freshman, asked Ali in seventh grade. Aria and the others had helped Ali get ready like she was Cinderella going off to the ball. Hanna was in charge of curling Ali's hair, Emily helped Ali into her ballerina-skirt dress, and Aria had the honor of clipping the diamond pendant Mrs. DiLaurentis had let Ali borrow for the night around her neck. Afterward, Ali bragged about her beautiful wrist corsage, the awesome music the DJ played, and how the dance photographer followed her around the entire time, telling her she was the most beautiful girl in the room. *As usual.*

Aria gazed bashfully at Noel. "Maybe that would be fun."

"It'll definitely be fun," Noel corrected her. "I promise." His piercing blue eyes softened. "And you know, the people at the Y are starting another group for general grief. Maybe you should go."

"Oh, I don't know," Aria said noncommittally, moving out of the way as Gemma Curran tried to shove her violin case into the adjacent locker. "I'm not really into the group therapy thing."

"Just think about it," Noel advised.

Then he leaned over, pecked Aria on the cheek, and left. Aria watched him disappear into the stairwell. Grief counseling wasn't the answer—she and her old friends had met with a grief counselor named Marion in January in an attempt to put Ali behind them, but it had only made them more obsessed.

The truth was, some niggling inconsistencies and unanswered questions about the case remained, things Aria still couldn't help thinking about. Like exactly how Billy knew so much about her and her friends—down to Spencer's family's dark secrets. Or what Jason DiLaurentis had said to Aria in the cemetery, after she accused him of being a psychiatric patient: *You've got it all wrong.* Only, *what* did Aria have wrong? Jason had obviously been an outpatient at the Radley, a mental hospital now turned classy hotel. Emily had seen his name all through the hospital's logbooks.

Aria slammed her locker shut. As she started down the hall, she heard a far-off giggle—*just like* the one she'd been hearing ever since she started receiving notes from A. She looked around, her heart slamming against her rib cage. The halls were thinning out, everyone scuttling off to homeroom. No one was paying any attention to her.

With trembling hands, Aria reached into her yak-fur bag and pulled out her cell phone. She clicked on the envelope icon, but there were no new text messages. No new clues from A.

She sighed. Of course there wasn't a new note from A—Billy had been arrested. And all of A's clues had been misleads. The case was solved. The pieces that didn't make sense weren't worth thinking about anymore. Aria dropped her phone back into her bag and wiped the sweat from her palms on her blazer. *A is gone,* she told herself. Maybe if she repeated it enough, she'd actually begin to believe it.

3

HANNA AND MIKE, POWER COUPLE

Hanna Marin sat at a corner table in Steam, Rosewood Day's chic coffee bar, waiting for her boyfriend, Mike Montgomery, to show up. It was the very last period of the school day, and both of them had it free. To prepare for the mini-date, Hanna flipped through the latest Victoria's Secret catalogue and folded down various pages. She and Mike liked picking which girls had the fakest boobs. Hanna used to play a version of the game with her now dead best friend turned maniac killer, Mona Vanderwaal, but it was *way* more fun playing it with Mike. *Most* things were more fun with Mike. The guys Hanna had dated in the past were either too prudish to look at nearly naked girls, or else thought making fun of people was mean. Best of all, thanks to being a member of the Rosewood Day varsity lacrosse team, Mike was more popular than all of them—even Sean Ackard, who'd gotten kind of preachy ever since he'd broken up with Aria and repledged his devotion to Virginity Club.

Hanna's iPhone chimed. She pulled it out of its pink leather case. On the screen was a new e-mail from Jessica Barnes, a local reporter. She was sniffing around for a quote for yet another Billy Ford story. *Thoughts about Billy's lawyer saying he's innocent? Reaction to the Polaroids of the four of you on the night Alison disappeared? Twitter me! J.*

Hanna deleted the message without replying. The idea that Billy was innocent was such bullshit. Lawyers probably *had* to say that about their clients, even if they were the biggest scumbags on earth.

Hanna had no comment on the creepy, hazy Polaroids from the night Ali went missing, either. She didn't want to think about that sleepover ever again for as long as she lived. Whenever she dared to dwell on Ali's, Ian's, or Jenna's murders—*or* the fact that Billy had stalked Hanna and her old friends—her heart pounded faster than a techno beat. What if the cops hadn't caught Billy? Would Hanna have been next?

Hanna gazed down the school hallway, wishing Mike would hurry up. A bunch of kids were leaning against the lockers, fiddling with their BlackBerrys. A squirrelly-looking sophomore boy was writing notes on his hand, probably for a test he had next period. Naomi Zeigler, Riley Wolfe, and Hanna's soon-to-be stepsister, Kate Randall, stood by a large oil painting of Marcus Wellington, one of the school's founders. They were laughing at something Hanna couldn't see, their hair shiny, their skirts shortened three inches above the knee, all of them wearing matching Tod's loafers and J.Crew patterned tights.

Hanna smoothed the new sapphire Nanette Lepore silk top she bought last night at Otter, her favorite store at the King James Mall, and ran her fingers down the length of her frizz-free auburn hair—she'd gone to Fermata spa this morning for a blowout. She looked perfect and glamorous, definitely not the kind of girl who'd spent any time in a mental hospital. Not the kind of girl who'd been tormented by her mentally ill roomie, Iris, or who'd spent a couple of hours in jail just two weeks ago. Definitely not the kind of girl anyone would exclude or ostracize.

But despite her flawless appearance, every single one of those things had happened. Hanna's father had warned Kate that she'd get in huge trouble if word got out about Hanna's stint at the Preserve at Addison-Stevens mental hospital. Billy-as-A had sent Hanna there, convincing Mr. Marin that it was the only proper treatment for post-traumatic stress disorder. All bets were off, though, when a photo of Hanna at the Preserve showed up in *People* magazine. A trip to the loony bin had made Hanna an instant social pariah, and she was ousted from the queen bee clique the second she returned to Rosewood Day. Not long after, Hanna discovered the word *PSYCHO* scrawled in Sharpie marker on her locker. Then she got a Facebook friend request from someone named Hanna Psycho Marin. Naturally, Hanna Psycho Marin had zero friends.

When Hanna complained to her father about the

page—she knew Kate was behind it—her dad just shrugged and said, "I can't force you girls to get along."

Hanna stood, straightened her clothes again, and elbowed through the mob. Naomi, Riley, and Kate had been joined by Mason Byers and James Freed. To Hanna's surprise, Mike was also with them.

"It's not *true*," he protested. There were pink splotches on his face and neck.

"Whatever, dude." Mason rolled his eyes. "I *know* this is your locker." He flashed his iPhone screen toward Naomi, Kate, and Riley. They groaned and squealed.

Hanna squeezed Mike's hand. "What's going on?"

Mike's gray-blue eyes were wide. "Someone sent Mason a photo of my lacrosse locker," he said sheepishly. "But they weren't mine, I swear."

"Sure, skidmarks," James teased.

"*Skidz*," Naomi quipped. Everyone tittered.

"What wasn't yours?" Hanna glanced briefly at Naomi, Riley, and Kate. They were still staring at Mason's iPhone. "What wasn't Mike's?" she repeated firmly.

"Someone's got a little skids problem," Riley chimed gleefully. The lax boys chortled and nudged each other.

"I *don't*," Mike protested. "Someone's messing with me."

Mason snorted. "You're messing *yourself*, more like it."

Everyone giggled again and Hanna grabbed the iPhone from Mason. On the screen was a picture of a Rosewood Day sports locker. Hanna recognized Mike's blue Ralph Lauren hoodie hanging from a hook, and nestled on the top shelf was his lucky Kellogg's Corn Flakes stuffed rooster. Front and center was a pair of white D&G boxer-briefs that were blatantly . . . skidded.

She slowly untangled her hand from Mike's and stepped away.

"I don't even *wear* D&G underwear." Mike stabbed at the screen, trying to delete the photo.

Naomi let out a screech. "Ew, Mason, Skidz touched your phone!"

"Purell!" James declared.

Mason took the phone from Hanna and held it tentatively between his thumb and forefinger. "Ugh. Skidz germs!"

"Skidz germs!" the girls echoed. A couple of blond, willowy freshman girls across the hall whispered and pointed. One of them took a picture with her camera phone.

Hanna glowered at Mason. "Who sent you this photo?"

Mason shoved his hands into the pockets of his pin-striped dress pants. "A concerned citizen. I didn't recognize the number."

Across the room, a poster for an upcoming French club food festival warped and wobbled before Hanna's eyes. It was just the kind of text A would have sent. But A was Billy . . . and Billy had been arrested.

"You believe me, right?" Mike took Hanna's hand again.

"Aw, they're holding hands!" Riley elbowed Naomi. "Skidz found a girl who doesn't mind his dirty undies!"

"Don't they make a cute couple?" Kate giggled. "Skidz and Psycho!"

The group exploded into jeering laughter. "I'm not a psycho," Hanna cried, her voice cracking.

The laughing continued unabated. Hanna looked around helplessly. A bunch of kids in the hall were staring. Even a student teacher ducked out of an earth science classroom and looked on with benign curiosity.

"Let's get out of here," Mike murmured in Hanna's ear. He wheeled around and stormed down the hall. His shoelace was untied, but he didn't stop to fix it. Hanna wanted to follow, but her legs felt fused to the polished marble floor. The giggles multiplied.

This was worse than the time in fifth grade when Ali, Naomi, and Riley called Hanna a "butterball" in gym, taking turns poking her stomach like the Pillsbury Doughboy. This was worse than when Hanna's presumed best friend in the world, Mona Vanderwaal, sent her a six-sizes-too-small court dress to wear to her birthday party—the dress split down the butt as soon as she walked in. Mike was supposed to be popular. *She* was supposed to be popular. And now they were both . . . freaks.

Hanna swept through the lobby and outside. The brisk February air bit at her nose and set the flags in the center of the green flapping angrily against the flagpole. They were no longer at half-mast, but a couple of people had placed flowers honoring Jenna and Ali at the base of the pole. Buses groaned into the drive and idled at the curb, ready for afternoon pickup. A couple of crows hunched under a spindly limbed willow tree. A dark shadow slid behind an overgrown shrub.

Goose bumps rose on Hanna's arms, the photo of her that had run in *People* popping into her mind. Hanna's crazy roommate at the Preserve, Iris, had taken it in a secret attic room whose walls were decorated with doodles from patients past. The drawing right behind Hanna's head, eerily close to her face, was a huge, unmistakable portrait of *Ali*. The girl in the drawing looked ominous and . . . alive. *I know something you don't*, the Ali on the wall seemed to say. *And I'm keeping a secret.*

Just then, someone tapped Hanna's shoulder. She screamed and whipped around. Emily Fields took a couple of defensive steps back, holding her hands in front of her face. "Sorry!"

Hanna ran her fingers through her hair, taking heaping breaths. "*God*," she groaned. "Don't *do* that."

"I had to find you," Emily said, out of breath. "I was just called into the office. Ali's mom was on the phone."

"Mrs. DiLaurentis?" Hanna wrinkled her nose. "Why would she bother you at school?"

Emily rubbed her bare hands together. "They're holding a press conference at their house right now," she said. "Mrs. DiLaurentis wants all of us to be there. She said she had something she needed to tell us."

An icy shiver wriggled up Hanna's spine. "What does *that* mean?"

"I don't know." Emily's eyes were wide and her freckles stood out on her pale skin. "But we'd better get over there. It's starting now."

4

THE BLOND BOMBSHELL

As the winter sun dipped low on the horizon, Emily sat in the passenger seat of Hanna's Prius, watching Lancaster Avenue fly by. They were speeding to Yarmouth, where the DiLaurentises now lived. Spencer and Aria were meeting them there.

"Make a right here," Emily instructed, reading from the directions Mrs. DiLaurentis had given her. They entered a subdivision called Darrow Farms. It looked like it had once been a real farm, with rolling green hills and lots of fields for crops and livestock, but a developer had subdivided it into identical plots of enormous homes. Each house had a stone facade, black shutters, and fledgling Japanese maples in the front yard.

It wasn't difficult to find the DiLaurentises' house—it had an enormous crowd at the curb, a large podium in the front yard, and swarms of cameramen, reporters, and producers. A phalanx of cops stood guard near the DiLaurentises' porch, most with intimidating black pistols on their belts. Many of the people in the throng were journalists, but there were definitely some curiosity-seekers, too—Emily spied Lanie Iler and Gemma Curran, two girls on her swim team, leaning against a sequoia. Spencer's sister, Melissa, loitered next to a Mercedes SUV.

"Whoa," Emily whispered. Word had spread. Whatever was happening must be huge.

Emily slammed the car door and started with Hanna toward the crowd. She'd forgotten to bring mittens, and her fingers already felt fat and jointless from the cold. She'd been scatterbrained about everything since Jenna's death, barely sleeping at night, hardly eating anything at meals.

"Em?"

Emily whirled around, signaling to Hanna that she'd catch up with her in a minute. Maya St. Germain stood behind Emily, wedged next to a boy in a Phillies snow hat. Under a black wool coat, Maya wore a striped boat-neck shirt, black jeans, and black leather ankle boots. Her curly hair was pinned back with a tortoiseshell clip, and her lips were coated in cherry-scented ChapStick. Emily spied a yellow wad of banana gum in her mouth, reminding her of the day she and Maya first kissed.

"Hey," Emily said cautiously. She and Maya weren't exactly on good terms—not since Maya had caught Emily kissing another girl.

Maya's lip quivered, and then she burst into tears. "I'm sorry," she blubbered, covering her face. "This is so hard.

I can't believe Jenna's . . ."

Emily felt a twinge of guilt. She'd seen Maya and Jenna together a lot lately—roaming the halls of Rosewood Day, walking through the atrium at the King James Mall, even at the diving competition of one of Emily's swim meets.

A tiny movement at the DiLaurentises' front window caught Emily's eye, distracting her. It looked like someone had parted the curtain, and then dropped it again. For a moment, she wondered if it was Jason. But then she noticed him near the podium, tapping on his cell phone.

She turned back to Maya, who was pulling a plastic Wawa bag from her army-green knapsack. "I wanted to give you this," Maya said. "The workers cleaning up the fire found it and thought it was mine, but I remember it from your room."

Emily reached into the bag and extracted a pink patent-leather change purse. A swirly initial *E* was inscribed on the front, and the zipper was pale pink. "Oh my God," she breathed. The pouch had been a gift from Ali in sixth grade. It had been one of the Ali artifacts Emily and her friends had buried in Spencer's backyard before Ian's trial. Their grief counselor claimed the ritual would help them heal from Ali's death, but Emily had missed the purse ever since.

"Thank you." She clutched it to her chest.

"No worries." Maya snapped her bag shut and slung it across her chest. "Well, I should go be with my family." She gestured through the crowd. Mr. and Mrs. St. Germain stood by the DiLaurentises' mailbox, looking a little lost.

"Bye." Emily faced front again. Hanna had joined Spencer and Aria near the barricades. Emily hadn't seen her old friends together since Jenna's funeral. Swallowing hard, she elbowed through the crowd until she was right next to them. "Hey," she said softly to Spencer.

Spencer looked at Emily uneasily. "Hey."

Aria and Hanna shrugged hellos. "How are you guys?" Emily asked.

Aria ran her fingers through the fringe of her long black scarf. Hanna stared at her iPhone, not answering. Spencer bit her bottom lip. None of them looked thrilled to be standing together. Emily turned the patent-leather change purse over in her hands, hoping one of her old friends would recognize it. She was dying to talk to them about Ali, but something had come between them ever since Jenna's body was found. It had happened after Ali disappeared, too—it was simply easier to ignore one another than to rehash the terrible memories.

"What do you think this is all about?" Emily tried again.

Aria pulled out a tube of cherry ChapStick and smeared it across her lips. "You were the one Mrs. DiLaurentis called. She didn't tell you?"

Emily shook her head. "She got off the phone really fast. I didn't have time to ask."

"Maybe it's about how Billy is claiming he's innocent." Hanna leaned on the barricade, making it sway a little.

Aria shivered. "I heard his lawyer wants the case

thrown out because they can't find a single boot print in Jenna's backyard. They don't have any physical evidence that links him to the scene."

"That's ridiculous," Spencer said. "He had all those photos of us, all those A notes. . . ."

"Isn't it kind of weird, though, that it turned out to be Billy?" Aria said in a low voice. She picked at a patch of dry skin on her thumb. "He came from out of nowhere."

The wind shifted, smelling pungently of cow manure from a nearby farm. Emily agreed with Aria; she had been certain that Ali's killer would end up being someone familiar, someone connected to her life. This Billy guy was a weird, random stranger who'd somehow dug up their deepest, darkest secrets. It could be done, Emily supposed—Mona Vanderwaal had unearthed tons of dirty secrets about Emily and the others just by reading Ali's abandoned diary.

"I guess." Hanna shuddered. "But he definitely did it. I hope they lock him up forever."

The microphone at the podium screeched with feedback, and Emily jerked her head up. Mrs. DiLaurentis, dressed in a sleek black sheath, a brown mink shrug, and black heels, emerged from the house. She fiddled with a stack of index cards. Her husband, looking even more gaunt and beak-nosed than Emily remembered, stood by her side. Emily also noticed that Officer Darren Wilden had appeared in the cluster of cops, his arms crossed tightly over his chest. Emily grimaced. Maybe Wilden hadn't killed his

Amish ex-girlfriend, but there was still something sketchy about him. Wilden hadn't believed in New A, even when they showed him the threatening missives. And he was so quick to discount the girls' sighting of Ali after the fire, making Emily and the others promise that they wouldn't say anything more about seeing her in the woods.

The crowd grew quiet. Flashbulbs snapped. "Rolling," a producer next to Emily whispered.

Mrs. DiLaurentis gave a watery smile. "Thanks for coming," she said. "The past four years have been very difficult and painful for our entire family, but we've had a lot of support. I want everyone to know that we're doing okay, and we're relieved to know that we can finally put our daughter's murder behind us."

There was a smattering of applause. Ali's mom continued. "Two tragedies have happened in Rosewood, to two very beautiful, innocent girls. I'd like all of us to have a moment of silence for my daughter and for Jenna Cavanaugh." She looked across the crowd at Jenna's parents, who were standing in an inconspicuous spot behind an oak tree. Jenna's mom's mouth was clenched, as though she was trying very hard not to cry. Jenna's father had his eyes trained stubbornly on an empty silver gum wrapper at his feet.

Emily heard a sniffle from the middle of the crowd, and then a loud *caw* of a crow. The wind whistled, shaking the bare trees. When she looked at the DiLaurentises' window, there was that flicker again.

Mrs. DiLaurentis cleared her throat. "But that isn't the

only reason I've called everyone here," she read from her note cards. "Our family has been hiding a secret for a long time, mostly for safety reasons. We think it's time to tell the truth."

It felt like a moth had gotten loose in Emily's stomach. *The truth?*

Mrs. DiLaurentis's mouth wobbled. She took a deep breath. "The truth is, we have another child. Someone who hasn't grown up always living with us because of . . ." She paused for a moment, nervously scratching the side of her nose. ". . . health issues."

The crowd began to murmur. Emily's mind swirled. *What* did Mrs. DiLaurentis say? She grabbed Aria's hand. Aria squeezed back.

Mrs. DiLaurentis shouted over the growing whispers. "Our daughter was recently released and given a clean bill of health, but we hoped to protect her from public scrutiny until her sister's true murderer was safely behind bars. Thanks to Officer Wilden and his team, that's now a reality."

She turned and nodded at Wilden, who ducked his head bashfully. A few people clapped. Emily tasted the peanut-butter-and-honey sandwich she'd had for lunch that day. *Daughter?*

"With that, we think it's time to introduce her to all of you." Mrs. DiLaurentis turned and signaled at the house. The front door opened. Out came a girl.

The change purse slipped from Emily's fingers. "*What?*"

Aria cried, dropping Emily's hand. Spencer clutched Emily's shoulder and Hanna slumped heavily against the barricade.

The girl on the porch had blond hair, porcelain skin, and a heart-shaped face. Her deep blue eyes landed on Emily's almost immediately. She held Emily's gaze, then winked. Emily's whole body turned to mush. "Ali?" she mouthed.

Mrs. DiLaurentis leaned into the microphone. "This is Courtney," she declared. "Alison's twin sister."

5

JUST WHEN YOU THOUGHT IT COULDN'T GET ANY CRAZIER

The murmurs rose to a roar and flashbulbs flickered furiously. A bunch of people started frantically texting. "A twin?" Spencer said weakly. Her hands trembled uncontrollably.

"Oh my God," Aria murmured, clapping her hand to her forehead. Emily blinked furiously at the girl, as if she didn't believe she was real. Hanna latched onto Emily's arm.

A portion of the crowd spun around and stared at Aria, Emily, Spencer, and Hanna. "Did they *know*?" someone whispered.

Spencer's heart fluttered hummingbird-fast. She *hadn't* known. Ali had kept lots of secrets from her—the clandestine relationship with Ian, her secret friendship with Jenna, the mystery of why she'd dumped Naomi and Riley for Spencer and the others in sixth grade—but a secret sister trumped all of those things.

She stared at the girl on the porch. Ali's twin sister was tall, her hair a little darker and her face a little narrower than Ali's, but otherwise she was identical to their old best friend. She wore black leggings, black flats, an oversize blue oxford shirt, and a cropped white jacket. A striped scarf was looped around her neck, and her blond hair was bunched into a bun. With her cupid's bow lips and sapphire blue eyes, she looked just like a French model.

Out of the corner of her eye, Spencer noticed her sister, Melissa, weaving through the crowd. Angling past the police barricades, she walked right up to Jason DiLaurentis and whispered something in his ear. Jason paled, turned toward Melissa, and said something back.

An uneasy feeling bolted through Spencer's stomach. Why was Melissa here? And what was she doing? She hadn't seen Melissa and Jason talk since high school.

Then Melissa craned her neck and stared at Courtney. Courtney noticed and flinched. Her smile drooped.

What the *hell*?

"What do you think about William Ford saying he's innocent?" A voice called out from the crowd, breaking Spencer's focus. The question came from a tall blond reporter in the front row.

Mrs. DiLaurentis pursed her lips. "I think it's reprehensible. The evidence against him is staggering."

Spencer turned back to Courtney. Dizziness overcame her. It was so *bizarre*. Courtney met her gaze, then shifted from Spencer to the other girls. Once she had everyone's attention, she signaled to the side door of the house.

Emily stiffened. "Does she want us to . . . ?"

"She couldn't," Spencer said. "She doesn't even know us."

Courtney leaned over and whispered something into her mom's ear. Mrs. DiLaurentis nodded, then smiled at the crowd. "My daughter is a little overwhelmed. She's going to go back inside for a while to rest."

Courtney turned for the door. Before she disappeared into the house, she looked over her shoulder and raised an eyebrow.

"Should we go?" Hanna said uneasily.

"*No!*" Aria gasped at the same time Emily said, "Yes!"

Spencer chewed on her pinkie. "We should see what she wants." She grabbed Aria's arm. "C'mon."

They sneaked around the side of the house, ducked past an overgrown holly bush, and darted through the red-painted side door.

The huge kitchen smelled of cloves, olive oil, and Febreze. One of the chairs was cocked at an odd angle to the table, as if someone had been sitting there moments before. Spencer recognized the old Delft pottery flour and sugar jars by the microwave from the DiLaurentises' old kitchen. Someone had started a grocery list and pinned it to the refrigerator. *Jelly. Pickles. French bread.*

When Courtney appeared from the hallway, a whisper

of a smile emerged on her eerily familiar face; Spencer's legs dissolved into Jell-O. Aria let out a small squeak.

"I promise I won't bite," Courtney said. Her voice was exactly like Ali's, husky and seductive. "I wanted a minute alone with you guys before things got too crazy."

Spencer nervously shaped her dirty blond hair into a ponytail, unable to take her eyes off the girl. It was like Ali had crawled out of the hole in her old backyard, grown back her skin, and become alive and whole again.

The girls all stared at one another, their eyes wide and unblinking. The clock on the microwave ticked from 3:59 to 4:00.

Courtney plucked a yellow bowl full of pretzels from the island and joined them. "You guys were my sister's best friends, right? Spencer, Emily, Hanna, Aria?" She pointed to each of them in succession.

"Yeah." Spencer curled her hands around the caning on her chair, remembering the time in sixth grade when she, Aria, Hanna, and Emily had sneaked into Ali's backyard, hoping to steal her Time Capsule flag. Ali had come out onto her porch, wearing a pink T-shirt and wedges, and caught them. After telling the girls they were too late—someone had already stolen the flag—she'd pointed at Spencer and said, "You're Spencer, right?" She then made the others introduce themselves, acting as if she was way too popular to remember their names. It was the first time Ali had ever spoken to any of them. Just one week later, she handpicked them as her new best friends.

"Ali told me about you." Courtney offered the girls pretzels, but everyone shook their heads. Spencer couldn't fathom eating right now. Her stomach had inverted itself.

"But she never told you about me, did she?"

"N-no," Emily croaked. "Not once."

"Then I guess this is pretty bizarre," Courtney said.

Spencer fiddled with a cork coaster that said MARTINI TIME! in fifties-style lettering.

"So . . . where were you? At a hospital or something?" Aria asked.

Not that Courtney looked sick. Her skin radiated, as if it was lit from an inside source. Her blond hair shone as if it was deep-conditioned hourly. As Spencer canvassed Courtney's face, a realization hit her with meteoric force: If Ali was Spencer's half sister, then this girl was, too. Suddenly she was keenly aware how much Courtney looked like Mr. Hastings . . . and Melissa . . . *and* Spencer. Courtney had her dad's long, slender fingers and button nose, Melissa's cerulean eyes, and the same dimple Spencer had on her right cheek. Nana Hastings had that dimple, too. It was amazing that Spencer hadn't noticed these similarities when Ali was alive. Then again, she hadn't known to look.

Courtney chewed thoughtfully. The crunches echoed through the room. "Kind of. I was at this place called the Radley. And then, after it became a hotel or whatever, I was moved to a place called the Preserve at Addison-Stevens."

She said the name with a haughty British accent, rolling her eyes.

Spencer exchanged a shocked look with the other girls. *Of course.* Jason DiLaurentis wasn't the patient at the Radley—*Courtney* was. His name was in the logbooks because he'd visited her. And Hanna had said that Iris, her roommate at the Preserve, had drawn a picture of Ali in some secret room. But Iris must have known Courtney, not Ali.

"So . . . it was for . . . mental issues?" Aria said tentatively.

Courtney pointed a pretzel at Aria like a dagger. "Those places aren't *just* for mental patients," she snapped.

"Oh." A bloom of red appeared on Aria's cheeks. "Sorry. I had no idea."

Courtney gave a shrug and stared into the pretzel bowl. Spencer waited for her to elaborate on why she *had* been in those facilities, but she said nothing.

Finally, Courtney raised her head. "Anyway. I'm sorry I ran away from you the night of the fire. That was probably really . . . confusing."

"Oh my God, that *was* you," Hanna exclaimed.

Spencer ran her fingers along the edge of the blue linen place mat. It made sense, of course, that it was Courtney who had emerged from the woods, not Ali's ghost or a figment from a weird group hallucination.

Emily leaned forward, her reddish-blond hair falling in her face. "What were you doing there?"

Courtney pulled her chair closer to the table. "I got a note—from Billy I guess—saying there was something in the woods I needed to see." Courtney's face twisted with remorse. "I wasn't supposed to leave the house, but the note said it would help solve Ali's murder. When I reached the woods, the fire started. I thought I was going to die . . . but then Aria saved me." She touched Aria's wrist. "Thank you, by the way."

Aria's mouth dropped open, but no sound came out.

"How did you get out of there so quickly?" Emily pressed.

Courtney wiped a stray piece of salt from her lip. "I called my contact at the Rosewood PD. He's an old family friend."

The sound of mic feedback filtered in from the press conference outside. Spencer gazed at Aria, Emily, and Hanna. It was obvious who the *family friend* was. It explained why they hadn't seen him the night of the fire. It also explained why he'd told them to stop saying they saw Ali the very next day: He'd needed to keep Ali's sister safe.

"Wilden." Emily's jaw tensed. "You shouldn't trust him. He's not what he seems."

Courtney leaned back, letting out an easy, amused chuckle. "Settle down, Killer."

A chilly frisson of fear slithered up Spencer's back. *Killer?* That was Ali's nickname for Emily. Had Ali told her?

But before any of them could say anything, Mrs. DiLaurentis appeared in the front hall. When she noticed the group, her face brightened. "Thanks for coming, girls. It means a lot to us."

Mrs. DiLaurentis walked over to Courtney and put her hand on her arm. Her long, perfect nails were painted classic Chanel red. "I'm sorry, honey, but there's someone from MSNBC who has a couple of questions. He's come all the way from New York. . . ."

"Okay," Courtney groaned, getting up.

"The Rosewood PD wants to speak with you, too," Mrs. DiLaurentis said. She took her daughter's face in her hands and began to smooth out Courtney's eyebrows. "Something about the night of the fire."

"*Again?*" Courtney sighed dramatically, wrenching away from her mom. "I'd rather talk to the press. They're more fun."

She turned back to the girls, who were still sitting motionless at the table. "Come by anytime, guys," she said, smiling. "Door's always open. And, oh!" She pulled a brand-new laminated school ID from her jeans pocket. COURTNEY DILAURENTIS, it said in big red letters. "I'm going to Rosewood Day!" she exclaimed. "See you at school tomorrow."

And then, with a final unsettling wink, she was gone.

6

FREAK NO MORE

The following morning, Hanna walked down the path from the student parking lot toward school. Channel 6, Channel 8, and CNN news vans were parked at Rosewood Day's main entrance. Reporters hunched behind the bushes like lions on the prowl. Smoothing her auburn hair, Hanna braced herself for their barrage of questions.

The reporter closest to her stared for a moment, and then turned to the others. "Never mind," he shouted. "It's only that Pretty Little Liar girl."

Hanna winced. *Only* that Pretty Little Liar girl? What the hell did that mean? Didn't they want to ask Hanna what she thought about Ali's secret twin? What about her opinions on Billy trying to prove his innocence? And while she was at it, how about a big, fat apology for all the mud they'd slung at her?

She stuck her nose in the air. Whatever. She didn't want to be on TV anyway. The camera added ten pounds.

A tubby guy operating the boom microphone

squawked into his Nextel walkie-talkie. Another reporter clapped her cell phone closed. "Courtney DiLaurentis is in the back parking lot!"

The reporters and camera people stampeded for the back of the school.

Hanna shuddered. *Courtney.* It hardly seemed real. The first few hours after Hanna left the DiLaurentis kitchen, she kept waiting for people with cameras to pop out of nowhere, announcing that this was all some bizarre prank.

Why hadn't Ali told them about her sister? All those sleepovers, all those notes between classes, all those trips to the Poconos and Newport. All those times they played Never Have I Ever or Truth or Dare, and Ali hadn't once spilled the secret. Should Hanna have sensed the truth when Ali wanted to pretend that they were quintuplets who'd been separated at birth? Or when she saw the drawing of Ali–*Courtney*–on the Preserve wall. Had Ali been dropping cryptic hints whenever she looked at Hanna and sighed, "You're so lucky to be an only child"?

Pushing past a knot of nerdy freshman girls watching a rerun of *Glee* on an iPhone, Hanna kicked open the front door and strutted inside. It looked like a Hallmark factory had thrown up in the lobby. The walls were slathered with white paper cupids, red heart-shaped streamers, and gold foil bunting. Next to the auditorium doors were giant candy-heart fixtures the school put up every year. FIND LOVE, said the first heart in wedding invitation–style calligraphy. AT THE VALENTINE'S BALL, said the second heart. THIS SATURDAY, said the final one. There were little bite marks in the corner of the last heart, probably from a rodent that had gotten into the storage closet where the hearts were kept for the rest of the year. Details about the dance were on pink flyers in a big woven basket, including the mandate that in honor of Valentine's Day, everyone must wear something red, pink, or white—even the boys. Because of the recent tragedy, ticket proceeds would go toward the newly established Jenna Cavanaugh fund, which would sponsor the training of Seeing Eye dogs. Interestingly, all traces of the Jenna Shrine that had been in the lobby yesterday had vanished. Either the Rosewood Day staff had gotten too many complaints of how depressing and disturbing it was, or now that Courtney was here, Jenna's death was yesterday's news.

A fit of giggles arose from Steam. Hanna turned and saw Naomi, Riley, and Kate sitting at one of the tile-topped café tables, nursing aromatic mugs of herbal tea and picking at warm cranberry-bran scones. There was a fourth girl there, too, with a heart-shaped face and huge blue eyes.

The milk steamer on the espresso machine hissed, and Hanna jumped. She felt transported back to sixth grade, when Naomi, Riley, and Ali had been joined at the hip. Of course it wasn't Ali sitting shoulder to shoulder with Naomi and Riley, looking as though they'd been friends forever. It was Courtney.

Hanna walked over, but just as she was about to sit

in the only empty chair at the table, Naomi plunked her enormous Hermès bag on the seat. Riley piled her green Kate Spade on next, and then Kate flung her studded Foley + Corinna hobo on top. The bags teetered like a Jenga tower. Courtney pressed her cranberry-colored tote to her chest, looking conflicted.

"Sorry, Psycho," Naomi said icily. "That seat's taken."

"I'm not psycho." Hanna narrowed her eyes. Courtney shifted in her seat, and Hanna wondered if the word *psycho* made her uncomfortable. *She'd* been in those hospitals, too.

"If you're not psycho," Kate teased, "then why did I hear you screaming in your sleep last night?"

The girls tittered. Hanna bit down hard on the inside of her cheek. If only she could somehow record this on her phone and show it to her father. Then again, would he even care? After the press conference, she'd waited for him to knock on her bedroom door to discuss what had happened. It used to be their regular thing—they'd talked for hours when Hanna didn't make junior cheerleading, when she worried that Sean Ackard would never like her, and when he and Hanna's mom decided to get a divorce. The knock never came, though. Mr. Marin had spent the evening in his office, seemingly unaware that Hanna was in major distress.

"Why don't you sit with Skidz?" Riley teased. The other girls cackled. "He's been waiting for you!" She pointed across the room.

Hanna followed Riley's bony, witchlike finger. Mike

was slumped at a back table right next to the bathroom, slurping from a tall paper cup of coffee and staring at a piece of paper. He looked like the only puppy at the pound who hadn't found an owner. Hanna's heart twisted. He'd sent Hanna a bunch of texts the previous night; she'd meant to write back, but she hadn't gotten around to it. She wasn't sure what to say. It didn't matter that the underwear in the photo wasn't his—everyone *believed* it was, just like everyone believed she was psycho. And nicknames stuck at Rosewood Day. In seventh grade, Ali had dubbed Peter Grayson "Potato" because he was shaped like Mr. Potato Head, and kids still called him that today.

Mike looked up and noticed her. His face brightened and he waved a pink flyer. On it were the words ROSEWOOD DAY VALENTINE'S DANCE.

She wanted to move closer to Mike's table, but if she sat with Mike—and especially if she agreed to go with him to the Valentine's Day dance—she'd be Psycho forever. Her little trip to the Preserve wouldn't be an unfortunate faux pas but a defining moment in her high school career. She wouldn't be on the A-list for house parties or picked for the prom committee—the *only* committee at Rosewood Day worth vying for. She wouldn't go with the right people to Jamaica or St. Lucia for spring break, which meant she wouldn't have a spot in the beach house in Miami during Junior Week in June. Sasha at Otter would stop holding clothes for her, Uri wouldn't be able to squeeze her in for last-minute highlights and blow-dries, and she'd transform back into dorky loser Hanna overnight—the weight would pile back on, Dr. Huston would put braces back on her teeth, and the LASIK eye surgery would suddenly stop working and she'd be stuck with the wire-rimmed, Harry Potter–style glasses she'd worn in fifth grade.

That *could not* happen. Ever since Ali rescued her from oblivion, Hanna had vowed to never, *ever* be a loser again.

Hanna took a deep breath. "Sorry, Skidz," she heard herself saying in a taunting and high-pitched voice that sounded nothing like her own. "I shouldn't get too close. Germs and all." She smirked.

Mike's lips parted. His skin paled as if he'd seen a ghost—the Ghost of Bitchiness Past, maybe. Hanna whirled around and faced Naomi, Kate, Riley, and Courtney. *See?* she wanted to scream. She could make sacrifices. She *deserved* to be part of their group.

Naomi stood and brushed muffin crumbs from her hands. "Sorry, Han, you may be Skidz-free, but you're *still* a freak." She re-knotted her Love Quotes silk scarf around her neck and beckoned the rest of the girls to follow. Riley fell in line behind her, then Kate.

Courtney remained at the table for a moment longer, her blue eyes glued to Hanna. "Your hair looks really pretty like that," she finally said.

Hanna touched her hair self-consciously. It looked the same as it usually did, blown out straight and styled with a dollop of Bumble & Bumble finishing serum. She thought again of that drawing Iris had done of Courtney on the attic wall, Courtney's eyes huge and haunting. A shiver ran up her spine. "Uh, thanks," she murmured cautiously.

Courtney held her gaze for a few minutes more, a weird smile on her lips. "You're welcome," she said. Then she slung her purse over her shoulder and followed the others down the hall.

7

NOEL KAHN, ROSEWOOD
WELCOME WAGON

A few hours later, Aria trudged into study hall, her third period of the day. It was held in a health classroom, which was adorned with posters describing the various symptoms of STDs, the havoc illegal drugs can wreak on your body, and what happens to your skin if you habitually smoke. There was also a heavy, waxy yellow blob at the back of the room that was supposed to represent what a pound of fat looked like in your body, and a long poster illustrating the various changes a fetus undergoes while in the womb. Meredith, Aria's pseudo-stepmother, was twenty-five weeks pregnant, and according to the Health chart, the fetus was about the size of a rutabaga. *Fun!*

Aria took a long sip of coffee from her thermal mug. She still ordered coffee beans from the little dive near where they'd lived in Reykjavík, Iceland. It cost a fortune just in shipping, but Starbucks didn't cut it anymore. Aria sat down as more students swarmed in. She heard a *clunk* nearby and looked up.

"Hey." Noel plopped into a seat across the aisle. Aria was surprised to see him—though Noel was technically in Aria's study hall, he usually spent the period in the school's weight room. "How are you doing?" he asked, his eyes wide.

Aria shrugged noncommittally, taking another hearty swig of coffee. She had a feeling she knew what Noel wanted to talk about. *Everyone* wanted to talk to her about it today.

"Have you talked to . . . you know, Courtney?" His lips twitched as he said the name.

Aria bit her thumbnail. "I talked to her a little. But hopefully I don't ever have to again."

Noel looked startled.

"What?" Aria snapped.

"It's just . . ." Noel trailed off, fiddling with one of the Absolut bottle–shaped key rings on his backpack. "I thought you'd want to get to know her, being that she's Ali's sister and all."

Aria turned away, staring at a brightly colored food pyramid display across the room. Her father, Byron, had said the same thing at dinner the previous night—that reaching out to Ali's long-lost sister might help Aria heal from Ali's death. Aria was pretty sure her mother, Ella, would say that, too, though she'd been avoiding her mom these days. Whenever she called Ella, she always ran the risk of getting her sleazy boyfriend, Xavier, instead.

The whole Courtney thing weirded Aria out: Courtney standing there at the podium, waving to the crowd. The DiLaurentises hiding her away for years without telling a soul. The press salivating at their every word. In the midst of the circus, Aria had glanced at Jason DiLaurentis. He had nodded along with everything his mom said, his eyes glazed like he'd been brainwashed. All remains of the burning crush Aria had on Jason vanished in an instant. He and his family were more messed up than she'd ever imagined.

Aria opened her bio book to a random page and pretended to read a passage on photosynthesis. Noel's eyes were on her, waiting. "It feels weird to be around her," she answered finally without looking up. "It brings back a lot of memories of Ali's disappearance and death."

Noel leaned forward, making the old wooden desk creak. "But Courtney went through that, too. Maybe it would be good for you guys to deal with it together. I know you're not into the group therapy thing, but talking with her could help."

Aria pinched the bridge of her nose. If anything, she needed group therapy to deal with Courtney's arrival.

A scuffle at the front of the room made her look up. Kids started to whisper. When Mrs. Ives, the study hall monitor, stepped away from the door, Aria's heart sank. Standing there was Courtney herself.

Mrs. Ives pointed Courtney to the only empty desk in the room, which was—of *course*—right next to Aria. Everyone in the class stared as Courtney started down the aisle, her hips swaying, her long blond hair swinging. Phi Templeton even snapped a quick picture of Courtney with her BlackBerry. "*She looks just like Ali,*" Imogen Smith hissed.

Courtney noticed Aria and brightened. "Hi! It's nice to see a friendly face."

"H-hey," Aria stammered. She had a feeling the expression on her face right now couldn't be categorized as *friendly.*

Courtney slid into the seat, slung her shiny reddish-pink tote over the chair, and removed a spiral-bound notebook and a purple pen from the front pocket. *Courtney DiLaurentis* was written across the front of the notebook in bubbly letters. Even her handwriting was identical to Ali's.

Bile rose in Aria's throat. She could *not* handle this. Ali was *dead.*

Noel twisted around and gave Courtney a huge smile. "I'm Noel." He extended his hand, and Courtney shook it. "Is this your first day?" he added as if he didn't know.

"Uh-huh." Courtney pretended to wipe sweat from her brow. "This place is crazy. I've never been to a school where so many classrooms are in barns!"

That's because you've never been to a real school, Aria thought, stabbing her mechanical pencil into a small indent in her desk.

Noel nodded enthusiastically, his face lit up like a Vegas slot machine. "Yeah, this place used to be a farm back in the day. At least the livestock aren't still here!"

Courtney tittered as if this was the funniest thing in the world. She angled her body ever so slightly toward Noel. Ali used to do the exact same thing with boys she liked—it was her way of marking her territory. Was it intentional? Some weird twin connection? Aria waited for Noel to tell Courtney that he and Aria were dating, but all he did was give Aria a righteous look. *See?* his expression said. *Courtney's not that bad.*

All of a sudden, a flood of bitter memories rushed back, fresh and sharp. In seventh grade, Aria told Ali that she had a crush on Noel. Ali assured her that she'd talk to him to see if he liked her back. But once she did, Ali told her, "Something kind of . . . *weird* happened at Noel's house. I told him about you, and he said he likes you as a friend. And then he said he likes *me*. And I think I like him back. But I won't go out with him if you don't want me to."

Aria had felt like her heart had been ripped from her chest and chopped into a billion pieces. "Um, okay," she said quickly. What could she say? It wasn't like she could compete with Ali.

Ali had gone on two dates with Noel—the first to see a chick movie of her choosing, the second to the King James Mall, where Noel waited patiently for hours while Ali tried on practically everything in Saks. Then, out of the blue, Ali broke up with Noel because she liked someone else—someone older. It must have been Ian.

And now history seemed to be repeating itself. Would Noel's feelings for Ali resurface now that her doppelgänger was here?

Courtney and Noel were still joking about the journalism barn, which contained a hayloft and a pig trough from the days of yore. Aria cleared her throat loudly. "Um, Noel, I had some thoughts about the Valentine's Day dance," she said. "Were you thinking about wearing a tux or a suit?"

Noel blinked, cut off in mid-sentence. "Uh, usually guys wear suits, I think."

"Cool," Aria said sweetly. She kept her eyes on Courtney the whole time, making sure Courtney understood Aria's intent. But instead of minding her business, Courtney pointed at something in Aria's yak-fur bag on the wood floor. "Hey! You still do that?"

Aria stared into the bag. Tucked in one of the big pockets was a tangled ball of white yarn and two wooden knitting needles. She snatched her bag from the floor and pressed it protectively to her chest. *You* still *do that?* That was a strange way to word it.

"My sister told me you knit," Courtney explained as if reading Aria's mind. "She even showed me a mohair bra you made for her."

"Oh." Aria's voice wobbled. The room suddenly smelled pungently of permanent marker and sweat. Courtney was gazing at her innocently and intently, but

Aria couldn't smile back. What *else* had Ali told Courtney about Aria? That she had been a kooky, friendless loser before Ali came along? That Aria had had a pathetic, teeming crush on Noel? Maybe Ali had even told her about the time they'd caught Byron and Meredith kissing in a parking lot. Ali had loved every minute of that—it was practically the only thing she talked to Aria about in the last few weeks before she disappeared.

Aria began to tremble. It was too much to sit here and pretend all of this was normal. When her Treo, which was sitting on the desk, let out a shrill chime, she nearly jumped out of her skin. A CNN news alert flashed across the screen. BILLY FORD MIGHT HAVE ALIBI.

Coffee gurgled in Aria's stomach. When she looked up, Courtney was staring intently at the alert, too, her eyes wide and her face pale. For a split second Courtney looked as though she wanted to rip the phone out of Aria's hands.

But in a blink, the look was gone.

8

SOME STRIPPING, NO TEASING

As Emily rushed to her Tuesday gym class, Aria caught her arm. "Look at this." She thrust her Treo into Emily's face.

On the screen was a recent newscast. "A critical and surprising development has arisen in the William Ford murder trial," a reporter's voice blared.

The camera cut to a shot of a convenience store parking lot. "A witness in Florida says he met with Mr. Ford outside this 7-Eleven on January fifteenth, the day the Pretty Little Liars discovered Mr. Ian Thomas's dead body in Rosewood," the voice-over explained. "The witness wishes to remain anonymous because the meeting had to do with the purchase of illegal drugs, but if investigators can corroborate the story, this alibi might be enough to exonerate Mr. Ford of Mr. Thomas's murder."

Mr. Owens, the strictest of the gym teachers, passed by, and Aria quickly slipped the phone in her pocket—they weren't supposed to use them during school hours. When he trundled around the corner, Aria played the video again. "How can this be possible?" she whispered, her face drawn. "If Billy was in Florida when Ian was killed, someone else must have taken those pictures and dug up that stuff on us as A."

Emily chewed nervously on her lips. "It doesn't make any sense. He's got to be lying. Maybe he paid someone to say that."

"With what money? He can't even afford a lawyer," Aria pointed out.

The two of them stood in silence for a few moments. Two guys on the wrestling team whipped past, playing some deranged version of hallway tag. The newscast ended, and the option to choose two more videos appeared on the screen. One was the report from the night Jenna was murdered. The other was about Courtney DiLaurentis. Emily stared at Courtney's picture, grief and confusion rippling through her once again. *Ali lied to us,* she thought, her heart breaking for the millionth time. Ali had left Emily and the others out of a huge part of her life. It was like they had never been friends at all.

Or *had* she dropped some hints? Ali had been obsessed with twins, for one thing—once, when Ali and Emily went shopping alone in Ardmore, Ali told everyone that they were twins, just to see how many people would believe them. And Ali used to marvel over how similar Emily and her sister Carolyn looked. "Has anyone ever thought you guys are twins?" she asked more than once. "Do people ever mistake you for each other?"

Aria noticed Emily looking at Courtney's picture. She touched Emily's wrist. "Be careful."

Emily flinched. "What are you talking about?"

Aria pursed her lips. A group of girls in cheerleading uniforms marched past, practicing the arm movements for a cheer. "She might look exactly like Ali, but she's not her."

Heat rushed to Emily's face. She knew what Aria was getting at. Emily's old friends knew about her crush on Ali—many of Emily's notes from the original A, Mona Vanderwaal, had talked about nothing else. Aria had accused Emily of letting her heart get in the way of her head before, especially when Emily clung to the idea that Ali was still alive.

"I know she's not Ali," she snapped. "I'm not an idiot." She whirled into the gym locker room without saying good-bye.

The room smelled of rubber sneakers, hair spray, and floral deodorant. A bunch of girls were already changing into their T-shirts and shorts, and the air was filled with chatter about the Valentine's Day dance that Saturday. Emily stomped to her locker, prickly with agitation. Aria had definitely hit a nerve.

Truth be told, Emily had lain awake all last night, reliving the moment Courtney had stepped onto the podium. Even though it wasn't *Ali*, Emily's heart had lifted when Courtney gave her that alluring wink. It had been thrilling to sit in the DiLaurentises' new kitchen, too, right across from this achingly beautiful, hauntingly familiar girl. Emily had dreamed about Ali for years; how could she *not* feel something for her identical twin?

And what did Aria mean, *be careful*? There was no reason to distrust Courtney—she'd been as much a victim in this as Emily and the others were. Courtney was lucky to have narrowly escaped the fire in the woods. Billy was obviously trying to kill her, too, just like he was trying to kill Emily, Aria, and the others.

But what if the newscast was right? What if Billy *hadn't* killed Ian or set that fire . . . or done anything else?

"Ahem."

Emily jolted up, the white T-shirt and blue shorts she'd pulled from her gym locker slipping from her hands. A blond girl with a heart-shaped face was sitting on one of the wooden benches at the end of the aisle. "Oh!" Emily cried, clapping her hand over her mouth. It was as if Courtney had appeared just because Emily had been thinking about her.

"Hi." Courtney was dressed in a snug-fitting Rosewood Day blazer, a white button-down, and a blue plaid skirt. Her school-issued blue socks were tight and even, stopping right below her pretty, diamond-shaped kneecaps. She stared at the gym clothes in Emily's arms. "I didn't know we were supposed to bring shorts and stuff."

"Yeah." Emily lifted her T-shirt by the collar. "You can get gym clothes at the school store." She cocked her head.

"Mr. Draznowsky didn't tell you that?" Mr. Draznowsky was their gym teacher.

"He just gave me this locker number and combination. I guess he assumed I knew what to do."

Emily lowered her eyes. Had Courtney ever attended a normal school? Had she ever been a member of a sports team, or played an instrument in band, or had to plot the best route to get to each class on time? Aria's words of caution gushed through Emily's mind again. Okay, so they didn't know Courtney, but what was Emily supposed to do, ignore her?

"Uh, I have an extra pair of shorts and a T-shirt," Emily offered, turning to her locker and digging to the bottom. She handed Courtney a swim T-shirt and a wrinkled pair of gym shorts. "The shirt isn't technically for gym class, but I think they'll let you slide for today."

"Oh my God, thank you." Courtney held the T-shirt at arm's length. It had a picture of a swimming pool and starting blocks. "*You rock the block*," she read aloud, then looked at Emily quizzically.

"My swim coach gave it to me for making captain this year," Emily explained.

Courtney's eyes widened. "Captain? Impressive."

Emily shrugged. She had mixed feelings about being captain of the swim team, especially since she'd considered quitting not so long ago.

Courtney spread out the gym shorts, noticing the school crest silkscreened near the hem. "What's this thing on the shield? A little penis?"

Emily burst out laughing. "That's a shark. Our mascot."

Courtney squinted. "A shark? Seriously?"

"I know. It looks more like a worm. Or a . . . penis." Emily felt funny saying the word aloud. "Now that you mention it, this freshman guy dresses up in a big foam shark costume at swim meets. And by the end, the top of the costume always gets kind of . . . *limp*."

A group of girls pushed their way out to the gym. Courtney leaned against the metal lockers. "This school is so weird. Penis sharks, that peppy music that's played between classes . . ."

"Don't get me *started* on that." Emily groaned. "Sometimes they forget to turn it off once the period begins. And it's, like, *blaring* while we're trying to take a math test. Did you meet Ms. Reyes from the office? She wears those big oval pink-tinted glasses?"

Courtney laughed. "She registered me."

"She's in charge of the PA music," Emily explained, talking over the sounds of a couple of toilets flushing in the bathrooms adjacent to the changing area. "And whenever the music runs long, I always picture her asleep at her desk."

"Either that or she's distracted because she's staring at the oil paintings she has of that little rat dog."

"That's her Chihuahua!" Emily laughed. "Sometimes she brings it to pep rallies. She made it a Rosewood Day blazer and skirt outfit—even though it's a boy!"

Courtney's shoulders shook with giggles. Emily's insides felt shiny and glowing. Courtney sat down on the bench and unbuttoned her blazer. "And I keep seeing lots of posters for a game called Time Capsule. What's *that* all about?"

Emily stared at a wad of green gum someone had stuck in the grout of the beige tiles on the wall. "It's just a stupid game," she murmured. Time Capsule was a longstanding Rosewood Day tradition, and by coincidence, the very first time Emily had ever entered Ali's backyard was when she'd tried to steal Ali's Time Capsule piece. Ali had been unusually friendly to them that day, telling Emily and the others that someone else had stolen it already. Emily had only recently learned that *someone* had been Jason. He'd then given it to Aria, who'd kept it hidden for years.

A *beep* sounded from inside Courtney's satchel. She pulled out her iPhone and rolled her eyes. "CNN *again*," she said dramatically. "They really want to interview me. I even got a call from Anderson Cooper himself!"

"Wow!" Emily grinned. Someone in one of the other aisles slammed their locker closed.

Courtney dropped her phone back in her bag. "Yeah, but I don't really *want* to talk to the press. I'd rather talk to you guys." She ran her hands along the initials *WD + MP* that someone had etched into the wooden bench. "You were with my sister the night she . . . the night that Billy . . . ?"

A shiver ran up Emily's spine. "Yeah. We were."

"It's so scary." Courtney's voice cracked. "To think he killed Jenna Cavanaugh and Ian. And he sent you all those awful notes."

The heat whirred on, sending little motes of dust swirling around the room.

"Wait a minute," Emily said suddenly, a thought occurring to her. "Billy sent me a picture of Ali, Jenna, and a blond girl. I thought it was Naomi Zeigler—but it was you, wasn't it?"

Courtney picked at a Chiquita banana sticker someone had affixed to the locker. "Probably. I met Jenna during my one visit here. She was the only person in Rosewood who knew about me."

Two girls in Rosewood Day gym shorts and tees strolled past Emily and Courtney, glancing at them briefly before looking away. Emily's mind whirled. So Jenna *had* known something, just like they'd suspected. Billy-as-A had also sent Emily to Jenna's house a few weeks ago so she could witness Jenna's fight with Jason DiLaurentis. Maybe they were arguing because Jason wanted to make sure Jenna kept the secret about Courtney. But what did that have to do with Billy?

The teacher banged on the door and called everyone to line up in their squads for indoor basketball. "God, I'm such a downer!" Courtney whispered, shaking her head ruefully. "Sorry I brought all this up. I'm sure it's weird to talk about it."

Emily shrugged. "We all should be talking about

it more." She faced Courtney, feeling brave. "And . . . well, if you ever have any questions about Rosewood—or anything else—I'm here."

Courtney brightened. "Really?"

"Sure."

"Maybe we could get together after school tomorrow?" Courtney asked, her face brimming with hope.

"Oh!" Emily started, surprised. The door to the gym swept open, momentarily filling the locker room with the sounds of shouts and bouncing basketballs.

"If it's too weird, that's okay," Courtney said quickly, her face falling. "With, like, Ali and stuff."

"No, getting together sounds great," Emily decided. "Want to come over to my house?"

"Okay," Courtney said.

Emily leaned down, untying her shoelace and then re-knotting it. Emily wanted to show more emotion, but she also felt embarrassed, like it would give away too much.

When Courtney cleared her throat, Emily looked up again and gasped. Courtney had pulled her blouse over her head and was standing in the middle of the aisle in her pleated skirt and a lacy pink bra. It wasn't like she was showing off . . . but she wasn't hiding, either.

Emily couldn't help but peek. Courtney's boobs were bigger than Ali's had been, but she had the same tiny waist. A million memories of Ali flashed through Emily's mind. Ali sitting in a bikini by the pool, Prada aviators perched on the tip of her nose. Ali lounging on Spencer's couch in gray terry-cloth boy shorts, her long, tanned legs crossed at the ankles. The feel of Ali's soft lips when Emily kissed her in the tree house. The excitement Emily felt in those heady seconds before Ali pushed her away.

Courtney turned, noticing that Emily was watching. One eyebrow arched slyly. A smile spread across Courtney's lips. Emily tried to smile back, but her lips felt like they were made of Gummi worms. Could Courtney know about the kiss? Had Ali told her? And was Courtney . . . flirting?

The main door to the locker room slammed again and Emily shot around the corner, finger-combing her reddish-blond hair in the full-length mirror. Courtney shut her locker, letting out a loud yawn. As Emily hustled for the door to the gym, Courtney caught her eye once more. She slowly closed one eye in a long, seductive wink, as if she knew exactly what she was doing . . . and exactly how it made Emily feel.

9

SECRETS, SECRETS EVERYWHERE

"Welcome to the Ruff House Grooming Salon!" a chipper woman in a red smock said to Spencer and Melissa as they guided the family's two labradoodles into the luxurious doggie spa. Grooming duty was usually Mrs. Hastings's job, but Mrs. Hastings couldn't even groom *herself* right now.

As the dogs stopped to sniff a large potted fern in the corner—and then lift their legs on it—Melissa let out a dramatic sigh and shot a resentful glance in Spencer's direction. Spencer grimaced. Okay, so Melissa still hated her for turning their mother into a catatonic agoraphobe. *Duly noted.* Did she have to ram it down Spencer's throat every chance she got?

A pigtailed groomer, who didn't look much older than Spencer, said she'd be with them in a few minutes. Spencer flopped down on a leather chair, and Beatrice slumped at her feet, chewing on one of the toes of Spencer's Kate Spade ballet flats.

Someone cleared her throat across the room. Spencer

looked up. A wild-haired old woman holding a teacup Chihuahua was giving her the stink eye. "You're that girl whose dead friend had a secret twin, right?" she said, pointing. When Spencer nodded, the woman made a *tsk* sound and pulled her dog close, as if Spencer were possessed. "Nothing good can come from that. *Nothing good.*"

Spencer's mouth fell open. "Excuse me?"

"Mrs. Abernathy?" a voice called from the hall. "We're ready for you and Mr. Belvedere." The old woman stood, shoving her dog under her arm. She gave Spencer a final foreboding look and disappeared around the corner.

Next to her, Melissa let out a baffled sniff. Spencer sneaked a tiny peek at her. As usual, her sister's chin-length hair was smooth and straight, her peachy skin was flawless, and her checkered wool coat was lint-free. All at once, Spencer was so sick of their stupid rift. If crazy old ladies in vintage Chanel had opinions about the bomb Mrs. DiLaurentis dropped yesterday, then certainly Melissa did, too. Ali wasn't the only one with a secret sister—Courtney was Spencer and Melissa's half sister, too.

"What do you think we should do about Courtney?" Spencer asked her.

Melissa dropped an organic dog biscuit back into a crystal bowl. "Pardon?"

"Courtney said that Ali told her a lot about us. Should I get to know her since . . . you know, we're related?"

Melissa looked away. "I didn't realize Ali and Courtney

were very close. What kind of stuff did she know?" She unscrewed the cap to her purple Nalgene bottle and took a long gulp.

Spencer felt an anxious pull in the pit of her stomach. "What did you say to Jason at the press conference, anyway?"

Melissa nearly choked on a mouthful of water. "Nothing."

Spencer clutched Beatrice's leash. Somewhere in the spa, a dog let out an unhappy yowl. It was clearly *not* nothing. "And since when are you friends with Jason? I haven't seen you two talk since high school."

The bells at the front door jingled, and a man walked in with an enormous poodle, a bandana around her neck. Both Rufus and Beatrice jumped to their feet, instantly alert. Spencer kept her eyes on her sister, determined not to back down until Melissa told her the truth.

Finally, Melissa sighed. "I was telling Jason that he should've told me that Courtney was back."

The New Age music that had been tinkling through the stereo suddenly went silent. "What do you mean 'back'? Did you *know* about Courtney?" Spencer whispered.

Melissa kept her eyes on her coat in her lap. "Um, kind of."

"For how long?"

"Since high school."

"*What?*"

"Look, Jason had this huge crush on me." Melissa

pulled Rufus toward her and stroked his head. "And one day, he blurted out that he had this secret sister who was in the hospital. He begged me not to tell anyone. It was the least I could do."

"What do you mean?"

A woman with two neatly groomed bichons frises passed. "Well, I kind of ditched Jason for Ian," Melissa said, not meeting Spencer's gaze. "I broke his heart."

Spencer tried to picture when it might have happened. Before the barn burned, she'd unearthed an old math notebook from when Melissa was in high school; inside was a note about Melissa and Jason hooking up. Spencer also remembered the Saturday after sixth grade started when she and her old friends had crept into Ali's yard to steal her piece of the Time Capsule flag. Two people had been fighting inside Ali's house—Ali screamed "Stop it!" and then someone else had mimicked her in a high-pitched voice. Next there was a crash, a loud *thump,* and then Jason had stormed out of the house. He stopped midway across the yard to glower at Ian and Melissa, who were on the Hastingses' deck. Melissa and Ian had started dating a few days before. . . .

If Melissa and Jason had had a fling, it must have been before that. Which meant Melissa had known that Ali had a secret twin even before Spencer and Ali became *friends.*

"Nice of you to say something," Spencer said through clenched teeth. The music clicked back on, this time with an old Enya song.

"I made a promise," Melissa said, wrapping Rufus's

leash around her hand so tightly it started to cut off her circulation. "It was Ali's place to tell you."

"Well, she didn't."

Melissa rolled her eyes. "Well, Ali was kind of a bitch."

The overpowering scent of eucalyptus dog toothpaste turned Spencer's stomach. She wanted to tell Melissa that *she* was a bitch, too. Screw protecting Jason—Melissa never protected anybody. No, Melissa had kept the secret because knowledge meant power and control—just like it had for Ali. Spencer's sisters were more alike than she'd ever realized. But Ali and Melissa weren't Spencer's only sisters.

Just days ago, she'd wished for an opportunity to start over with Ali without manipulation, lies, or competition. She'd never have that chance, but maybe she had the next best thing.

Without a word, Spencer handed Melissa Beatrice's leash and stormed out of the salon.

When Spencer pulled up to the DiLaurentises' new home, she was relieved to find that the news vans, cop cars, and barricades from the press conference yesterday were gone. It looked like a normal house again, identical to all the other houses except for the staircase over the garage, which led to Jason's studio apartment.

Spencer climbed out of the car and stood very still. A snowblower grumbled in the distance. Three crows sat on a green electrical box across the street. The air smelled like spilled motor oil and snow.

Rolling her shoulders, she walked up the gray flagstone path and rang the DiLaurentises' bell. There was a *thud* from inside. Spencer hopped from foot to foot, wondering if this was a mistake. What if Courtney didn't know they were related—or didn't care? Just because Spencer wanted a sister didn't mean she'd get one.

Suddenly the door flung open, and Courtney appeared. Spencer gasped involuntarily. "What?" Courtney asked sharply. Her eyebrows made a V.

"Sorry," Spencer blurted. "It's just . . . you look so . . ."

Here was Ali, exactly as she was in Spencer's memory. Her blond hair was wild and wavy over her shoulders, her skin gleamed, and her blue eyes sparkled under a fringe of thick, long eyelashes. There was such a disconnect in Spencer's mind—this girl *looked* just like Ali, and yet she wasn't her old friend.

Spencer waved her hands in front of her face, wishing she could shut the door and start this all over again.

"So, what's up?" Courtney said, leaning against the doorjamb. There was a hole in her left red-and-white-striped sock.

Spencer chewed her lip awkwardly. *God, she even sounded like Ali.* "There's something I want to talk to you about."

"Cool." Courtney ushered Spencer in, then turned and padded down the hall toward the stairs. Framed photos of the DiLaurentis family lined the walls. Spencer recognized many of them from the DiLaurentises' old house. There was the picture of the family on a double-decker bus in London, a black-and-white one of them on a beach in the Bahamas, and the fish-eye-lens photo of them in front of the giraffe habitat at the Philadelphia Zoo. The familiar images took on new significance as Spencer followed the unpictured DiLaurentis through the house. Why hadn't Courtney gone on any of the vacations? Had she been too sick?

Spencer stopped in front of a photo she didn't recognize. It was of the family on the back porch of their old house. Mother, father, son, and daughter grinned broadly, happily, as if they didn't have a secret in the world. It must have been close to the time Ali went missing—there was a big bulldozer looming in the yard, near where the gazebo was going to be. There was another shape at the edge of the property, too. It looked like a person. Spencer leaned close, squinting, but couldn't quite make out who it was. Courtney cleared her throat, waiting on one of the upper steps. "Coming?" she asked, and Spencer scuttled away from the photos, like she'd been caught spying. She sprinted up the stairs.

There were lots of moving boxes in the upstairs hallway. Spencer dug her fingers into her palm when she saw one labeled *Ali—Field Hockey*. Courtney skirted around a purple Dyson vacuum and pushed through a door at the end of the hall. "Here we are."

When Spencer saw the room, she felt as though

she'd stepped back in time. She recognized the hot-pink bedspread immediately—she'd helped Ali pick it out at Saks. There was the big black Rockefeller Center subway station sign that Ali's parents had bought for her at an antique store in SoHo. And the license-plate mirror over the bureau was the most familiar of all. Spencer had given it to Ali on her thirteenth birthday.

These were Ali's things, all of them. Didn't Courtney have any possessions of her own?

Courtney flopped down on the bed. "What's on your mind?"

Spencer sank into the paisley, stuffed chair across the room and straightened the protective arm covers so the patterns matched up. This wasn't something she could drop on a person without warning—especially someone who'd spent her life battling a mysterious illness. Maybe this was a bad idea. Maybe she should just up and leave. Maybe . . .

"Let me guess." Courtney picked at a loose thread on the duvet. "You want to talk about the affair." Courtney shrugged. "Your dad. My mom."

Spencer gasped. "You know?"

"I've always known."

"But . . . how?" Spencer cried.

Courtney's head was down, and Spencer could see her jagged part and perfectly honey-blond roots. "Ali found out. And then she told me on one of her visits."

"*Ali* knew? Billy wasn't just making that up?" Billy-as-

Ian had IM'ed Spencer about the affair right before he'd killed Jenna.

"And she never told you, right?" Courtney clucked her tongue.

A sparrow landed on the ledge of Courtney's window. The room smelled suddenly of new carpet and fresh paint. Spencer blinked hard. "Do Jason and your dad know?"

"I'm not sure. No one's ever said anything. But if my sister knew, my brother probably does, too. And my parents pretty much hate each other—which means my dad is probably clued in." She rolled her eyes. "I swear they only stayed together because Ali went missing. I'll bet you that a year from now they divorce."

Spencer felt a tangerine-size lump in her throat. "I don't even know where my dad *is* right now. And my mom just found out about this. She's really messed up."

"I'm sorry." Courtney looked straight at Spencer.

Spencer shifted her weight, and the chair squeaked angrily. "Everyone was keeping things from me," she said quietly. "I have an older sister, Melissa. You may have seen her at the press conference. She was talking to your brother." *She was also the one who glared at you,* she wanted to add.

"Melissa told me she's known that Ali had a twin since high school," Spencer continued. "She never bothered to mention it to me. I'm sure she loved knowing something I didn't. Some sister, huh?" She let out a loud, clumsy sniff.

Courtney rose, plucked a Kleenex box off the bedside

table, and plopped down at Spencer's feet. "She sounds really competitive and insecure," she said. "That's how Ali was with me, too. She always wanted the limelight. She hated if I was better at anything. I know she was pretty competitive with you, too."

That was an understatement. Spencer and Ali used to compete over everything—who could bike to Wawa the fastest, who could kiss the most older guys, or who could make JV field hockey in seventh grade. There were lots of times Spencer didn't want to race, but Ali always insisted. Was it because Ali knew they were also sisters? Was she trying to prove something?

Salty tears spilled down Spencer's cheeks, and sobs rose in her chest. She wasn't even sure what she was crying about. All the lies, maybe. All the hurt. All the deaths.

Courtney pulled her in and hugged her tight. She smelled like cinnamon gum and Mane 'n Tail shampoo. "Who cares what our sisters knew?" she murmured. "The past is the past. We have each other now—right?"

"Uh-huh," Spencer murmured, still choking on sobs.

Courtney pulled away, her face brightening. "Hey! Want to go dancing tomorrow?"

"Dancing?" Spencer wiped her puffy eyes. Tomorrow was a school night. She had an AP history test at the end of the week. She hadn't seen Andrew in days, and she still needed to get a dress for the Valentine's Day dance. "I don't know. . . . "

Courtney grabbed her hands. "C'mon. It'll be our

chance to break free of our evil sisters! It's like that 'Survivor' song!" And then she leaned back and launched into the old Destiny's Child song. "'I'm a sur-*vi*-vor!'" she sang as she waved her hands over her head, stuck out her butt, and wheeled around crazily. "Come on, Spencer! Say you'll go dancing with me!"

Despite all her grief and confusion, Spencer burst out laughing. Maybe Courtney was right—maybe the best thing to do amidst all this craziness was kick back, let go, and have a good time. This was what she'd wanted, after all—a sister she could confide in, rely on, and have fun with. Courtney seemed to want the same exact thing.

"Okay," Spencer said. And at that, she let out a big breath of air, stood up, and sang along with her sister.

10

A TICKET TO POPULARITY

A few hours later, Hanna maneuvered her Prius up the winding driveway, turned off the engine, and grabbed two shopping bags from Otter from the passenger seat. She'd made an emergency, I-feel-sorry-for-myself trip to the King James Mall after school today, though it wasn't much fun shopping without a BFF or Mike. She didn't trust her judgment anymore, either, and she wasn't sure if the ultra-skinny Gucci leather pants she'd purchased were disco-fabulous or just plain slutty. Sasha, Hanna's favorite salesgirl, had said Hanna looked great in them . . . but then again, she got commission on the sale.

It was pitch-black outside, and a thin crust of frost had formed over the front yard. She heard a giggle. Her heart started to hammer. Hanna paused in the driveway. "Hello?" she called. The word seemed to freeze right in front of her face before shattering into thousands of shards on the driveway. Hanna looked right and left, but it was too dark to see anything.

There was another giggle, and then a full-throated laugh. Hanna exhaled with relief. It was coming from inside the house. Hanna crept up the front walk and slipped quietly into the foyer. Three pairs of boots sat by the front door. The emerald Loeffler Randalls were Riley's—she had a thing for green. Hanna had been with Naomi when she bought the spike-heeled booties lying next to them. Hanna didn't recognize the third pair at all, but when she heard another peal of giggles from upstairs, one girl's laugh stood out from the rest. Hanna had heard an identical version of that laugh many times, sometimes at her expense. It was Courtney. *And she was in Hanna's house.*

Hanna tiptoed up the stairs. The hallway smelled of rum and coconut. An old Madonna remix blared from Kate's closed bedroom door. Hanna approached and pressed her ear to the wall. She heard whispering.

"I think I saw her car pull into the driveway!" Naomi hissed.

"We should hide!" Riley cried.

"She'd better not try and hang out with us," Kate scoffed. "Right, Courtney?"

"Um," Courtney said, not really sounding certain at all.

Hanna padded to her bedroom and resisted the urge to slam the door behind her. Dot, her miniature Doberman, rose from her doggie bed and danced around her feet, but she was so angry that she barely noticed her. She should've seen this coming. Courtney had become

Naomi, Kate, and Riley's pet project, probably because she was the new media darling. All day, they'd prowled the Rosewood Day hallways in an intimidating four-girl line, flirting with the cutest boys and rolling their eyes at Hanna whenever she crossed their path. By eighth period, students were no longer looking at Courtney with uneasiness but respect and admiration. Four guys had asked her to the Valentine's Day dance. Scarlet Rivers, a finalist in the fashion design department's *Project Runway* contest, wanted to design a dress with Courtney as her muse. Not that Hanna was stalking Courtney or anything. It had all been on Courtney's brand-new Facebook page, which had already amassed 10,200 new friends from around the world.

There was a chime, and Hanna's iPhone lit up inside her bag. She pulled it out. *One new e-mail,* said the screen. The note was from her mom. Hanna rarely heard from her—Ms. Marin ran the Singapore division of McManus & Tate, an ad agency, and she was more in love with her career than her only daughter. *Hey, Han,* it began. *I've been offered six tickets to the Diane von Furstenberg fashion show in NYC Thursday, but I obviously can't use them. Would you like to go instead? I've attached them via PDF.*

Hanna read the message a few times over, her fingers twitching. *Six tickets!*

She stood up, checked her reflection in the mirror, and whipped out into the hall. When Hanna pounded on Kate's door, the giggles instantly ceased. After some heated whispers, Kate flung open the door. Naomi, Riley, and Courtney were sitting on the floor by Kate's bed, dressed in jeans and oversize cashmere sweaters. Bottles of foundation and trays of eye shadow were strewn across the carpet, and there was the usual array of *Vogues*, old Rosewood Day yearbooks, and smartphones jumbled at their feet. Four small tumblers and a bottle of Gosling's rum sat between them. Mr. Marin had brought the rum back from a recent business trip to Bermuda. Even if Hanna ratted Kate out for swiping it, her dad would probably somehow figure out a way to blame Hanna instead.

Riley's forehead wrinkled. "What do *you* want, Psycho?"

"Would you mind keeping it down?" Hanna cooed sweetly. "I need to make a phone call about some fashion week tickets I got from my mom, and I can hear your voices all the way down the hall."

It took a few seconds for the news to sink in. "What?" Kate squeaked, curling her lip.

Naomi tossed her head. "*Fashion* week? *Right.*"

"Just turn the music down for a few," Hanna said. "I don't want Diane von Furstenberg's people to think I'm a silly high school girl." She waggled her fingers and ducked out the door. "Thanks much!"

"Wait." Kate grabbed Hanna's arm. "*The* Diane von Furstenberg?"

"You have to be someone to have tickets to that," Riley snapped, her nostrils flaring. She had the tiniest beginning of a booger up her nose. "They don't let psychos in."

"My mom got six tickets," Hanna said nonchalantly, swiveling on her heel. "She gets stuff like that through her job all the time. But since she's in Singapore, she gave them to me."

She whipped out her iPhone, opened the PDF, and shoved it in Kate's face. Everyone else sprang up and squinted at the screen. Naomi licked her lips hungrily. Riley shot Hanna her version of a genuine smile, which looked more like a grimace. Courtney lingered in the background, her hands in the back pockets of her jeans. The other girls turned to her in deference, as if she were Anna Wintour and they were Assistants One through Three.

"Sweet," Courtney declared in a voice identical to Ali's.

Naomi clapped her palms together. "You're obviously bringing your besties, right?"

"Of course she's taking us," Riley said, linking her arm with Hanna's.

"Yeah, Hanna, you know that Psycho stuff was a joke, right?" Kate simpered. "And you should totally hang out with us tonight. We were *going* to ask you, but we didn't know where you were."

Hanna unwound her arm from Riley's. She had to play this very, very carefully. If she gave them what they wanted too quickly, she'd look like a pushover. "I'll have to think it over," she said apathetically.

Naomi let out a whine. "Come *on*, Hanna. You have to take us. We'll do anything."

"We'll take down that Facebook page," Riley blurted.

"We'll clean Psycho off your locker," Naomi said at the exact same time.

Kate nudged both of them, obviously not wanting them to *admit* they'd been behind those things. "*Fine*," she grumbled. "From now on, you're no longer Psycho."

"Oh, okay. Whatever," Hanna said lightly. She started to head for the door.

"*Wait!*" Naomi screeched, pulling Hanna back down by the sleeve of her blazer. "Are you taking us or not?"

"Mmmm . . ." Hanna pretended to think. "Okay. I guess."

"*Yes.*" Naomi and Riley high-fived. Kate looked appeased. Courtney gazed at them as if she thought this was all very petty. They made arrangements to meet Thursday after school at Hanna's car, when they'd drive to the Amtrak station. And where would they get dinner after the show? The Waverly Inn? Soho House?

Hanna left them to their planning and ducked into the hall bathroom, closing the door tight. She leaned over the sink, nearly knocking over Kate's myriad bottles of cleansers, toners, and mud masks, and smiled at her reflection. She'd *done* it. For the first time in weeks, she felt like herself again.

When she opened the bathroom door a few minutes later, a figure jerked out of sight. Hanna halted, her heart jumping to her throat. "Hello?" she whispered weakly.

There was a rustling sound. Then Courtney stepped

into the light. Her eyes were round, and there was a ghostly smile on her lips.

"Uh, hi?" The hairs on Hanna's arms stood on end.

"Hey," Courtney said. She walked up to Hanna, stopping inches from her face. The hallway seemed even darker than it had moments before. Courtney was so close that Hanna could smell her rum-scented breath.

"Um, I heard you knew Iris." Courtney tucked a strand of pale blond hair behind her ear.

Hanna's stomach did a flip. "Uh, yeah."

Courtney put her hand on Hanna's arm. Her fingers were ice-cold. "I'm so sorry," she whispered. "She was out of her mind. I'm glad you got away from her, too."

Then Courtney slid back into the shadows. Her bare feet made no sound on the plush carpet. The only way Hanna could tell she was still there was by the glowing ticking hands on her Juicy Couture wristwatch. Hanna watched the eerie green glow glide down the hall until it vanished, ghostlike, into Kate's room.

11

A SYMPATHETIC EAR

After school the following day, Aria screeched into the parking lot of the Rosewood YMCA, an old mansion that still maintained an English-style garden and a giant carriage house that had once held twenty Rolls-Royces. Mr. Kahn had needed Noel's SUV for the afternoon, and Aria had offered to pick Noel up from his Wednesday afternoon support group. She was also dying to tell Noel about the slinky, twenties-style red dress she'd found at a vintage store in Hollis this afternoon. Silly as it was, the Valentine's gala was the first school-sponsored dance Aria had ever attended, and she was surprised by how excited she was.

She maneuvered around the big parking lot, veering so as not to hit a Mercedes SUV whose driver was backing out of a space without bothering to check behind him. Suddenly the Grateful Dead song on the college radio station went silent. "We have an update on the Rosewood Serial Killer," a reporter broke in. "Billy Ford, the alleged murderer in custody, claims he has an alibi for both the night Alison DiLaurentis went missing *and* the night Jenna Cavanaugh was killed. Police will look thoroughly into these findings. If his lawyers can prove his alibis, he may be able to go free. This will open up what investigators thought was an airtight case."

The double doors to the Y opened wide, and Aria looked up. A crowd spilled down the massive stone steps. Two people walked apart from the others, deep in conversation. Aria recognized Noel's dark hair right away. The person with him had a mane of blond hair. When she pushed her hair behind her ear, Aria gasped. It was Courtney.

She wanted to duck, but Noel had already spied the Subaru and was on his way over. Courtney followed. Aria watched them approach helplessly, feeling like a firefly caught in a jar.

"Hey," Noel said, opening the passenger door. "You wouldn't mind driving Courtney home, too, would you? Her mom's supposed to pick her up, but she called and said she was going to be really late."

Courtney waved at Aria sheepishly, lingering a safe distance away. Aria scrambled for an excuse, but she couldn't come up with anything fast enough. "Fine," she muttered.

Noel mouthed *Sorry*. But he didn't look particularly sorry. He shut the front door and clambered into the backseat, beckoning for Courtney to follow. Anger surged into Aria's chest—were they both going to sit in the back and make Aria look like a *chauffeur*?

But then Courtney opened the front passenger door and slid in next to Aria. Aria tried to meet Noel's eyes in the mirror, but he was typing on his iPhone. Was this his way of getting them to bond? Hadn't she already told him that being around Courtney brought back too many unhappy memories?

The first mile was quiet. They passed the empty playground, an organic restaurant, and the entrance to the Marwyn running trail. Courtney sat prim and straight in her seat; Noel pounded away on his keyboard. Finally, Aria couldn't stand it anymore. "So you're both in the sibling support group, huh?"

"I told Courtney that she should check it out," Noel said. "I said it helped me."

"I see." Aria resisted the urge to drive the car into the icy duck pond on their left. When had Noel and Courtney had *that* conversation?

Noel leaned his elbows on the backs of the front seats. "Do you like it, Courtney? I think the counselor is really cool and down-to-earth."

"A little *too* down-to-earth," Courtney laughed. "'Now, fall back into your partner's arms!'" she imitated, using a deep, dopey voice. "'The idea is to trust someone else as much as you would trust a tree or a brook.'" She snorted. "You were totally about to drop me, too."

"I was not!" Noel insisted. His cheeks were pink.

Aria clenched her teeth. "You guys were partners?"

"Well, yeah. We're the youngest ones there by far." Noel switched his STX baseball cap so that the brim faced backward.

"Noel saved me from being partners with a randy old man with hair growing out of his ears," Courtney said, turning her head to smile at him.

"How *chivalrous* of you, Noel," Aria said frostily. She wasn't going to make him feel better about flirting with Ali's look-alike. Courtney wasn't exactly innocent, either— Aria had made it clear in study hall that she and Noel were an item, and yet she had no qualms about hanging all over him. Like sister, like long-lost twin.

"You can drop me first." Noel finally broke the silence. His street was coming up on the left.

"Are you sure?" Courtney asked, looking distressed. Aria wondered if she didn't want to be alone with Aria any more than Aria wanted to be alone with her.

"No worries," Noel said. Aria didn't answer, digging her nails so hard into the leatherette steering wheel that they left little half-moon-shaped dents.

When they pulled up to the gate at Noel's house, Courtney gaped at the Kahns' half-stone, half-brick mansion with its towers and four chimneys. Her eyes swept from the expansive side yard, which went on for another quarter mile over a series of small hills, to the guesthouse behind the mansion, to the detached garage, which held Mr. Kahn's antique car collection and Cessna airplane. "You live *here*?" she gasped.

"It's not that great inside," Noel mumbled. He climbed out of the car and walked over to Aria's side. He looked repentant. *Good.* She rolled down the window. "Can I call you later?" he said softly, touching Aria's arm. Aria nodded begrudgingly.

Courtney shifted in her seat as they pulled away. Aria considered turning up the radio, but what if they broke in with yet another news bulletin about Billy? She certainly didn't want to get into a discussion about *him*. "The bypass is the quickest way to Yarmouth, right?" she said stiffly, her eyes on the road.

"Right," Courtney said quietly.

"Okay then." Aria made a jerky right onto the highway, almost jumping the curb.

They drove past a huge parking lot for the local Barnes & Noble and Fresh Fields grocery store. Aria stared straight ahead, pretending to be fascinated by the COEXIST bumper sticker on the Honda in front of her. Each of its letters was comprised of a different religious symbol. She could feel Courtney watching her, but she didn't take the bait. It was like the Buckingham Palace Guard game Aria and Mike used to play on long, boring car trips: Aria would stare straight ahead like a palace guard while Mike tried to make her laugh.

Courtney took a deep breath. "I know what you're thinking. What everyone's thinking."

Aria broke from her spell and shot Courtney a brief,

puzzled look. "Um . . ."

Courtney continued, her voice low. "Everyone is wondering how I coped, living so far away from my family for so long. They want to know how I can forgive my family for keeping me out of the loop all those years."

"Uh," Aria wavered. Truthfully, she *was* thinking that.

"But that's really not my biggest problem," Courtney continued. "What's worse is that my parents are basically living this lie, pretending their issues don't exist." She turned to face Aria. "Did you know my mom had an affair?"

Aria got too close to the Honda in front of her and slammed on her brakes. "You knew about that?"

"Yeah. Ali and I both knew for years. And what's more, my dad isn't *even* my dad. Surprise!" Courtney laughed wearily. Her voice was thick, as if she was about to cry.

"Huh." Aria pressed on the gas and whipped past a white BMW, then a red Jeep Cherokee. The speedometer said she was doing almost eighty, but it felt like she was standing still. Spencer had told her about her dad's affair—*and* that she was Ali and Courtney's half sister. But she'd had no clue that *Ali* had known about the affair.

Aria took the exit off the highway into Yarmouth. The sign for Darrow Farms loomed ahead. Aria would never forget the day she and Ali caught Byron and Meredith making out in the Hollis parking lot. Ali had relentlessly teased Aria about the affair, talking about it as if it was a celebrity scandal on *TMZ*. *Has anything happened at home?* said Ali's texts. *Does Ella suspect? Remember the look on your dad's face when he caught us? You should look through his stuff to see if he's written his girlfriend any love letters!*

Ali had tortured Aria, but all that time she'd been going through the exact same thing.

Aria glanced over at the girl in the passenger seat. Courtney had her head down and was fidgeting with a beaded bracelet on her right wrist. With her hair over her face and her bottom lip stuck out ever-so-slightly, she looked much more fragile and weaker than Ali ever had. Much more innocent, too.

"A lot of parents are messed up," Aria said softly.

A few brown, dead leaves swirled past the car. Courtney pressed her lips together, her eyes narrowed. For a moment, Aria was afraid she'd said the wrong thing. She pulled into the DiLaurentises' driveway, and Courtney quickly opened the car door. "Thanks again for the ride."

Aria watched as Courtney ran across the yard and disappeared into the house. She remained at the curb for a few moments longer, her thoughts swarming. She certainly hadn't expected *that* conversation.

She was about to shift into drive when the hair on the back of her neck stood on end. It felt like someone was staring at her. Aria swiveled around and peered into a dark knot of trees across the street. Sure enough, someone was standing there, her eyes on Aria's car. The figure disappeared into the woods fast, but not before Aria caught a quick glimpse of a head of pale blond hair, cut bluntly at the chin. She gasped.

It was Melissa Hastings.

12

DREAMS REALLY DO COME TRUE

Late Wednesday afternoon, Emily stood in front of her bedroom mirror, turning first to the right, then to the left. Should she have used a curling iron on her stick-straight, reddish-blond hair? Did her sister Carolyn's pink lip gloss look stupid? She pulled off the striped T-shirt she was wearing, threw it on the floor, and slid on a pink wool-cashmere sweater instead. That looked wrong, too. She checked the digital clock on the nightstand again. Courtney would be here any minute.

Maybe she was overthinking this. Maybe Courtney hadn't even been flirting with her in gym class. She had been in unconventional schools her whole life—she might not be well-versed in the fine art of flirtation and other social cues.

The doorbell rang, and Emily froze, staring at her wide-eyed expression in the mirror. In an instant, she was thundering down the stairs and scampering through the hall to the door. No one else was home—her mother had taken Carolyn to a doctor's appointment after swimming, and her dad was still at work. She and Courtney would have the house to themselves.

Courtney stood on the steps, her cheeks pink and her blue eyes sparkling. "Hey!"

"Hi!" Emily unintentionally backed away just as Courtney came in for a hug. Then Emily stepped forward to hug, too, just when Courtney was self-consciously stepping aside.

Emily giggled. "Come in," she said. Courtney shuffled into the foyer and looked around, taking in the hutch of Hummel figurines in the hall, the dusty, upright piano in the living room, and the cluster of hanging plants that Mrs. Fields had brought indoors for the winter.

"Should we go to your room?"

"Sure."

Courtney bounded up the stairs, turned right at the landing, and stopped at the door to the bedroom that Emily and Carolyn shared. Emily gawked. "H-how did you know where my room was?"

Courtney gave her a crazy look. "Because it says so on your door." She pointed at the wooden sign that said EMILY AND CAROLYN in cartoonish letters. Emily let out a breath. *Duh.* It had been there since she was six.

Emily moved some stuffed animals off her twin bed so they could both fit. "Wow," Courtney breathed, gesturing at the Ali collage over the bureau. It was a series of photographs of Emily and Ali together from sixth and seventh grade. In one corner was a shot of the five of them in the living room of Ali's Poconos house, doing each other's hair. In another corner was a photo of Emily and Ali in matching striped bikinis on Spencer's pool deck, their arms wrapped around each other's shoulders. There were plenty of pictures of Ali alone, many of which Emily had snapped without Ali knowing—of Ali sleeping on Aria's rollaway cot, her face relaxed and beautiful. Another of Ali sprinting up the hockey field in her Rosewood Day JV uniform, her stick raised high in the air. Propped up next to the collage was the patent leather change purse Maya had returned to her at the press conference. Emily had scoured all the dirt and grime off it as soon as she'd gotten home that afternoon.

Emily blushed, wondering if the shrine was weird. "That stuff is so old. I haven't gone through it in a long time." *It's not like I'm obsessed or anything,* she wanted to add.

"No, I like it," Courtney insisted. She bounced on the bed. "It looks like you guys had a lot of fun."

"Yeah," Emily said.

Courtney flung off her Frye boots. "What's that?" She pointed at a jar on Emily's nightstand.

Emily cradled the jar between her palms. The contents rattled. "Dandelion seeds."

"What for?"

Color rushed to Emily's cheeks. "We all tried to smoke them once, to see if we'd hallucinate. It's stupid."

Courtney crossed her arms over her chest, looking

intrigued. "Did it work?"

"No, but we *wanted* it to work. So we put on music and started to dance. Aria made these squiggly motions in front of her face, like she was seeing shapes. Hanna stared at her fingerprints, like they were really fascinating. I giggled at everything. Spencer was the only one who didn't play along. She kept saying, 'I don't feel anything. I don't feel anything.'"

Courtney leaned forward. "What did Ali do?"

Emily jiggled her knees, suddenly shy. "Ali . . . well, Ali made up this dance."

"Do you remember it?"

"It was a long time ago."

Courtney poked Emily's leg. "You *do* remember it, don't you?"

Of course she did. Emily remembered pretty much everything Ali did.

Wriggling with glee, Courtney clasped Emily's hands. "Show it to me!"

"No!"

"Please?" Courtney begged. She was still holding Emily's hands, which made Emily's heart beat faster and faster. "I'm dying to know what Ali was really like. I hardly saw her. And now that she's gone . . ." She broke her gaze, staring absently at the poster of Dara Torres that hung over Carolyn's bed. "I wish I'd known her for real."

Courtney looked at Emily with clear blue eyes so much like Ali's that the back of Emily's throat burned.

Emily pressed her hands to her knees and stood. She shifted from left to right, then shimmied her shoulders up and down. After about three seconds of dancing, she blurted out, "That's all I can remember," and went to sit down fast. But her left foot stumbled over her fish-shaped slippers next to the bed. As she groped for balance, her hip rammed into the bed frame. "Oof," she said, hurtling face-first toward Courtney's lap.

Courtney grabbed Emily's waist. "Whoa," she giggled. She didn't let go right away. Pulsing heat sizzled through Emily's veins.

"Sorry," Emily mumbled, shooting up to stand.

"No worries," Courtney said quickly, straightening her plaid shirt.

Emily sat back down on the bed and looked anywhere else in the room besides Courtney's face. "Oh! It's four fifty-six," she blurted stupidly, pointing to the digital clock by the bed. "Four-five-six. Make a wish."

"I thought that was only for eleven eleven," Courtney teased.

"I make up my own rules."

"It seems that way." Courtney's eyes gleamed.

Emily felt suddenly breathless.

"Tell you what," Courtney chuckled. "I'll make a wish if you do."

Emily shut her eyes and lay back on the bed, her body throbbing from the fall and her head reeling from the smell of Courtney's skin. There was something she really wanted to wish for, but she knew it was impossible. She tried to think of random wishes instead. For her mom to finally let her paint her side of the bedroom a color other than pink. For her English teacher to give her a good grade on the F. Scott Fitzgerald paper she'd handed in that morning. For spring to come unnaturally early that year.

Emily heard a sigh and opened her eyes. Courtney's face was inches from hers. "Oh," Emily breathed. Courtney moved even closer. The room vibrated with possibility.

"I . . ." Emily started, but then Courtney leaned forward and touched her lips to Emily's. A billion explosions went off in Emily's head. Courtney's lips were soft yet firm. Emily's mouth fit hers perfectly. They kissed deeper, pressing harder. Emily was pretty sure her heart was beating even faster than it did in a fifty-meter freestyle sprint. When Courtney broke away, her eyes were shining.

"Well, I got *my* wish," Courtney said giddily. "I always hoped I'd get to do that again."

Emily's mouth tingled. It took her three long beats before she realized what Courtney said. "Wait . . . *Again?*"

Courtney's smile turned shaky. She bit her bottom lip and grabbed Emily's hand. "Okay. Don't freak out. But Em . . . it's me. *Ali.*"

Emily dropped Courtney's hand and moved a few inches away. "I'm sorry. What?"

Courtney's eyes were glassy, as if she was about to cry. Light from the corner window spilled across her face, making her look both angelic and ghostly. "I know it's crazy, but it's true. I'm Ali," she whispered, lowering her head. "I've been trying to figure out how to tell you."

"To tell me that you're . . . Ali?" The words felt leaden on Emily's tongue.

Courtney nodded. "My twin's name was Courtney. But she didn't have health problems. She was certifiably insane. In second grade, she started imitating me, pretending to *be* me."

Emily scuttled backward until her spine hit the wall. The words weren't exactly making sense.

"She hurt me a couple of times," Courtney went on, her voice strained. "And then she tried to kill me."

"How?" Emily whispered.

"It was the summer before third grade. I was in the pool in our old house in Connecticut. Courtney came out and started dunking me. At first, I thought it was a game, but she wouldn't let me up. While she held me underwater, she said, 'You don't deserve to be you. I do.'"

"Oh my God." Emily curled into a ball, gripping her knees to her chest tightly. Out the window, a flock of birds took off from the roof. Their wings flapped fast, as if they were fleeing something terrifying.

"My parents were horrified. They sent my sister away and moved the family to Rosewood," the girl across from Emily whispered. "They told me never to talk about her, which is why I kept her secret. But then in sixth grade, Courtney switched from the Radley to the Preserve. She put up this huge fight about it—she didn't want to start over at a new hospital—but once she was there, she finally began to improve. My parents decided to have her live at home for the summer after seventh grade on a trial basis. She came back a few days before the school year ended."

Emily opened her mouth, but no words came out. Courtney had been here in seventh grade, too? But Ali and Emily were friends then. How had Emily missed her?

Courtney—or was it Ali?—gave Emily a knowing look, as if she understood what Emily was thinking. "You guys saw her. Remember the day before our sleepover when I found you on the patio, but you said you'd just seen me upstairs in my room?"

Emily blinked fast. Of course she remembered. They'd caught Ali in her bedroom, reading a notebook. Mrs. DiLaurentis had appeared and sternly told the girls to go downstairs. Minutes later, when Ali found them in the backyard, she'd acted as if the incident in the bedroom had never happened. She had on a completely different outfit, and she seemed startled that Emily and the others were there, like she'd had no memory of the past ten minutes.

"That was Courtney. She was reading my journal, trying to be me again. After that, I stayed away from her. The night of our sleepover, Spencer and I fought, and I ran out of the barn. But Billy didn't attack me like everyone thinks—I ran back to my bedroom, and he . . . well, he got the wrong sister."

Emily put her hand over her mouth. "But . . . I don't

understand. . . ."

"My sister was supposed to stay in her bedroom all night," Courtney—no, Ali—went on. "When my parents saw only me the next morning, they assumed I was Courtney—*Ali* was supposed to be in Spencer's barn. I tried to tell my parents that *I* was Ali, but they didn't believe me—that was Courtney's act. *I'm Ali, I'm Ali,* she always said."

"Oh my God," Emily whispered. The peanut butter crackers she'd eaten earlier roiled in her stomach.

"Then when the twin they thought was Ali didn't come home from the sleepover, they flipped out. They figured I was Courtney, and that I had done something terrible. They couldn't handle having a sick daughter home while the other was missing, so they sent the girl they thought was her back to the Preserve the next afternoon. Except . . . it was *me*." She placed her palm over her heart, her eyes filling with tears. "It was *horrible*. They didn't visit me once. Jason used to visit Courtney all the time, but even he wouldn't listen to me when I pleaded that I was Ali. It was like a light switch went off in their heads and I was dead to them."

The neighbor's rattling Honda Civic passed. A dog barked, then another. Emily stared at the girl across from her. The girl who claimed to be *Ali*. "But . . . why didn't you call us before they shipped you off?" Emily asked. "We would've known the truth."

"My parents wouldn't let me use the phone. And then at the hospital, I wasn't allowed to make any calls. It was like being in prison." Tears streamed down Ali's face. "The more I said I was Ali, the sicker everyone thought I was. I realized that the only way to get out was to act like I really *was* Courtney. My parents still don't know who I am. If I tell them, they might send me back." She hiccupped. "I just want my life again."

Emily offered her a Kleenex from a box on her nightstand, and then took one herself. "So whose body did the police find?"

"Courtney's. We're twins, so we have the same DNA. We even have the same dental records." She gazed at Emily in grief and desperation. "I remember everything about you, Emily. *I* was the one who did that dance when we smoked the dandelion seeds. *I'm* the one in these photos on your wall. I remember how we met, and I especially remember you and me, in my tree house, kissing."

The smell of vanilla soap filled Emily's nostrils. She closed her eyes, practically seeing the stunned look on Ali's face after she'd kissed her. She and Ali had never directly discussed it. There were plenty of times Emily had wanted to, but she'd been too afraid. Ali had started teasing her about it so quickly afterward.

"I was talking about an older boy I liked," Ali rehashed, "and then suddenly, you kissed me. I got all self-conscious and scared, but then you wrote that note to me. The one that said how much you liked me. I loved it, Em. I'd never gotten a note like that from anyone in my life."

"Really?" Emily traced a heart into her duvet cover. "I

figured you thought I was a freak."

Ali winced. "I was scared. And stupid. I acted like an idiot. But I had almost four long years in the hospital to think it over." She placed her palms on her knees. "What more do I need to say to make you believe me? What can I do to prove that *I'm* Ali?"

Emily's lips still tingled from the kiss, and her hands and legs were trembling with shock. But as stunning as this was, she'd known, deep down, that something about Courtney was amiss. She'd felt that special spark between them, like they'd known each other for years. And they *had*.

Emily had dreamed of this moment for years. She'd consulted horoscopes and tarot cards and numerological charts, desperate for a clue that Ali was alive. She'd saved every single one of Ali's notes, random doodles, and just-'cause-I-feel-like-it gifts, unable to let them go because a deep, mystical force inside her urged that this wasn't over. Ali was still out there. She was okay.

And all this time, Emily had been right. She'd been granted her biggest wish of all.

The clouds lifted from her head. Emily's heart banged out a constant, steady beat, clear and pure. She gave Ali a wobbly smile. "Of course I believe you," she said, throwing her arms around her old friend. "I'm so glad you came back."

13

BLAST FROM THE PAST

Spencer adjusted the scoop neck of her Milly halter dress and flashed a fake ID to a bald bouncer at Paparazzi, a two-story club in Old City, Philadelphia. The bouncer studied it, nodded, and handed it back to Spencer. *Sweet.*

Next came Courtney, dressed in a gorgeous gold minidress. Courtney showed the bouncer an old fake ID of Melissa's, and the bouncer nodded her through. Emily pulled up the rear, looking surprisingly sexy in a red A-line dress, a bold beaded necklace, and strappy silver heels she'd borrowed from Courtney's closet. Courtney had called Spencer an hour before they were supposed to leave for their big night out, saying that she and Emily had really hit it off and that she wanted to invite Emily to go dancing with them. Spencer didn't mind—now that she'd bonded with Ali's twin, she wanted everyone else to love her just as much.

Emily handed the bouncer her older sister's fake ID, and after the bouncer nodded inattentively and handed it back, the three of them pushed inside. "We are going to have an awesome time," Courtney said, grabbing their hands. "I am *so* excited."

"Me too," Emily said, giving Courtney a long, meaningful look. Spencer couldn't help but smirk. It looked like Emily's crush on Ali had transferred over to her twin sister.

It was crowded for a Wednesday night. The club was in an old bank with marble pillars, intricate woodwork, and a mezzanine level that looked over the dance floor. A Black Eyed Peas song was playing at a deafening volume, and a bunch of college-age kids were writhing around enthusiastically, not caring that they had no rhythm—or that they were spilling their drinks all over themselves. The place smelled overwhelmingly like beer, cologne, and too many bodies in too small a space. A bunch of guys turned when they saw Spencer and her friends, their eyes instantly zeroing in on Courtney's blond hair, her slim hips, the way her dress skimmed her thighs. Everyone knew who she was. It was a wonder the news vans hadn't arrived yet.

Courtney leaned over the bar and ordered them three raspberry martinis. She returned with three pinkish drinks. "Bottoms up, ladies."

"I don't know . . ." Spencer said uncertainly.

"Yeah!" Emily said at the same time. Spencer gaped at her. Who *was* this girl, and what had she done with the old Emily?

"You're outvoted!" Courtney grinned. "Ready, set, chug!"

Spencer good-naturedly tilted the drink to her lips, letting the tart liquid spill down her throat. When she finished, she wiped her mouth and let out a whoop.

The others finished their drinks, too, and Courtney flagged down a seven-foot-tall bartender who looked suspiciously like a drag queen. "Let's dance!" she said after handing them their second rounds. They shimmied toward the dance floor and began to gyrate to "Hollaback Girl." Courtney stretched her arms over her head and closed her eyes. Emily swayed back and forth to the beat.

Spencer leaned forward and shouted in Emily's ear. "Remember those dance contests we used to have in Ali's living room?" They moved all the furniture to the corners, cranked up the stereo, and made up elaborate dance moves to Justin Timberlake. "This is just like that . . . only better."

Emily gave Spencer a coy look. "More than you know, actually."

Spencer frowned. "What do you mean?" But Emily took a long swig of her drink and turned away.

The crowd around them thickened. Spencer felt people staring. A bunch of guys edged close, taking advantage of every opportunity they could to bump against Courtney's hips, Emily's long legs, or Spencer's bare shoulders. Girls looked on longingly, many of them waving their arms over their heads like Courtney was, hoping some of her magic would rub off on them. The wallflowers sitting in booths gaped at the three of them as if they were Hollywood starlets.

Euphoria washed over Spencer. The last time she'd felt this amazing was right after Ali had befriended all of them at the Rosewood Day Charity Drive, first inviting them for smoothies at Steam, then asking them to a sleepover at her house. Spencer had no idea why Ali had chosen her out of all the rich, pretty sixth graders at Rosewood Day—she hadn't even made Spencer compete for her attention. When Spencer had returned to her charity booth after the smoothie, her peers had gazed at her enviously. Everyone wanted to be in Spencer's shoes, just like they did now.

Dappled light from the disco ball slithered across the length of Courtney's body as she moved. A dark-haired guy started to writhe against her. He was a few inches shorter than Courtney, wore a tattoo-tee, and sported an ironic, hipsterish mustache. He reminded Spencer of an emo version of a Super Mario Brother.

Courtney pointedly turned away from him, but he wouldn't take no for an answer. Next he ground against Emily's hip. Emily looked mortified. Spencer nudged between them, grabbing Emily's hands and twirling her around. Mario vanished through the crowd, but in seconds he was back, his eyes now on Spencer.

"Hide behind me," Courtney squealed. Spencer tipsily ducked behind her. Emily moved closer, doubled over in laughter. Mario danced by himself a few feet away, his movements bizarre and jerky. Every so often he glanced at the three of them, clearly hoping they'd invite him into their circle.

"I think one of us has to dance with him to make him go away," Emily said.

Courtney put her finger to her lips. She glanced at Emily and smiled mischievously. Then, Courtney tipped her head toward Spencer. "Not it."

The words sank in slowly. Spencer suddenly tasted sticky martini at the back of her throat. "W-what?"

"Not it," Courtney repeated, still bobbing to the beat. Even her eyes danced. "Don't tell me you've forgotten our old favorite game, Spence."

Our old favorite game? Spencer stepped away from Courtney, nearly colliding with a tall girl with waist-length brown hair. Lightning crackled through her veins. Something was wrong here. Very, very wrong.

Emily and Courtney exchanged another knowing look. Then Courtney took Spencer's arm and guided her and Emily away from the dance floor to a quieter part of the bar. Spencer's heart rocketed. Something about this seemed planned, staged.

They made her sit down in an empty booth. "Spence, I have something to tell you," Courtney said, pushing a lock of hair out of her face. "Emily already knows."

"Knows?" Spencer repeated. Emily smiled conspiratorially. "Knows what? What's going on?"

Courtney reached out and grabbed her hands. "Spence. I'm *Ali*."

Spencer's head snapped up. "That's not funny."

But Courtney had a serious look on her face. Emily did, too.

The music warped. The strobe light was giving Spencer a migraine. She slid farther into the booth. "Stop it," she demanded. "Stop it right now."

"It's true," Emily said, her eyes wide and unblinking. "Honest. Just hear her out."

Courtney began to explain what had happened. When Spencer heard the word *switch*, the martinis she'd downed crawled up the back of her throat. How was this possible? She didn't believe it. *Couldn't* believe it.

"How many times were you two in Rosewood together?" Spencer croaked, woozily gripping the edge of the banquette.

"Just once," Courtney—Ali?—said, her eyes downcast. "The weekend my sister died."

"No, wait." Emily frowned, raising a finger. "Wasn't she here one other time?" She reached into her black patent clutch, pulled out her phone, and showed them the old photo text A had sent. Ali, Jenna, and a third blond girl whose back was to the camera stood in the DiLaurentises' yard on what looked like a late-summer afternoon. The third blond girl could definitely be Ali's twin.

"Oh." Courtney pushed her hair out of her eyes and snapped her fingers. "Right. I forgot. She was home for a couple hours when she was switching hospitals."

Spencer counted the funky glass tiles on the wall along

the back of the booth, trying to make some sense and order out of the chaos. "But if Courtney always pretended she was Ali, how do I know *you* aren't Courtney?"

"She's *not*," Emily urged. The blond girl shook her head, too.

"But what about the ring?" Spencer pressed, pointing to Courtney's naked finger. "The girl in the hole was wearing Ali's initial ring on her pinkie. If you're Ali, why was Courtney wearing it?"

Courtney made a pinched face, as if she'd done a shot of Sour Apple Pucker schnapps. "I lost the ring the morning before our sleepover. I'm sure my sister stole it."

"*I* don't remember you wearing it that night," Emily said quickly.

Spencer shot Emily a look. Of course Emily wanted to believe this was Ali—this was what she'd wanted for the past four years. But as Spencer struggled to remember, she wasn't sure, either. *Had* Ali worn her ring the night of their sleepover?

A bunch of spiky-haired guys in button-downs passed by, looking as though they wanted to approach and hit on them, but they must have sensed something weird was going down and ambled away. Courtney took Spencer's hands. "Remember that day we fought in the barn? I've thought about that for three and a half years. I'm so sorry. And I'm sorry about other stuff I did, too— like hanging my JV hockey uniform in my window so you'd see. I *knew* it got to you. But I was jealous . . . and insecure. I always worried that you deserved to be on the hockey team, not me."

Spencer clutched the seat of the leather-upholstered booth, trying to breathe. *Anyone* could've known about the fight in the barn—Spencer had had to relay that information to the police. But the hockey uniform in the window? That was something Spencer hadn't even told her friends.

"And I'm sorry about all that stuff with Ian, too," Courtney—or was it really Ali?—said. "I shouldn't have said I was going to tell Melissa you two had kissed when *I* was the one in a relationship with him. And I shouldn't have said that I'd made him kiss you. That wasn't even true."

Spencer gritted her teeth, all the shameful, angry feelings from that fight bubbling up again. "Gee, thanks."

"I was bitchy, I know. I felt so bad afterward that I didn't even bother to meet Ian. I ran up to my room instead. So in a way, *you* saved me, Spence. If we hadn't had that fight, it would have been me out there in the woods, easy prey for Billy." Ali wiped her eyes with a cocktail napkin. "And I'm sorry I didn't tell you I knew we were sisters. I only found out a little bit before our last sleepover, and I didn't know how to deal with it."

"How did you even find out?" Spencer asked weakly.

The music changed to a Lady Gaga song and the whole bar erupted into cheers around them. "It doesn't really matter, does it?" she said. "What matters right now is what

I said to you yesterday at my house—I want to start fresh. To be the sisters we've always wanted."

The room spun wildly. There was a clamoring, greedy crowd three-deep at the bar. Spencer stared at the girl sitting across from her in the booth, scrutinizing her small, pink hands, her round fingernails, and long neck. *Could* this be Ali? It was like looking at a very well-made knockoff Fendi bag, trying to distinguish it from a real one. The differences had to be there.

And yet . . . it made sense. Spencer had had a funny feeling the moment this girl had stepped onto the stage at the press conference that something was . . . *off*. The secret twin had looked at all of them so knowingly. She'd called Emily *Killer*. She'd decorated her room exactly as Ali had. She'd gotten every element of Ali right, something even a good impersonator—even a *twin*—couldn't pull off. This was the girl who'd befriended her that day of the charity drive. The one who'd made her feel wanted, special.

But then she thought about the eerie photographs Billy had taken the night of the sleepover. If only Ali would have let Spencer open the blinds, if only she hadn't insisted on doing everything her way, they would've seen who was out there. None of this might have happened.

"We spent every day together for two years. How come you never told us about your sister?" Spencer asked, lifting her hair off the back of her neck. It seemed like a hundred more people had just entered the bar. She felt trapped and panicky, like the time she and Melissa got stuck in an overstuffed Saks elevator on Black Friday.

Ali blew her blond bangs off her face. "My parents asked me not to. And also . . . I was ashamed. I didn't want you guys to ask all kinds of uncomfortable questions."

Spencer let out a frustrated sniff. "Like the kinds of questions you used to ask us?"

Ali stared at her helplessly. Emily pulled her bottom lip into her mouth. The music throbbed in the background.

"You knew all our secrets," Spencer said, her voice trembling. Her anger was accumulating fast, like a snowball that grew bigger and bigger as it rolled down a hill. "You held them over us for power. You were afraid that if we knew this, we'd hold it over you. You wouldn't have any leverage anymore."

"You're right," Ali conceded. "I guess that's true. I'm sorry."

"And why didn't you try to contact us from the hospital?" Spencer went on, her skin pulsing with fury. "We were your best friends. You should have said something. Do you have any idea what we went through after you vanished?"

Ali's mouth did acrobatics as she tried to assemble a response. "I . . ."

Spencer cut her off. "Do you have any clue how hard that was?" Tears were now streaming down her face. A couple of people gaped at her as they passed, then scuttled on.

"It was hard for me, too!" Ali protested, shaking her

head. "I wanted to tell you guys, I swear! I didn't contact you at first because I *couldn't*. It took me months to get phone privileges, and by the time I could call you, eighth grade had started. I thought . . . well, after all I did to you guys, you wouldn't want me back anyway." She gazed stubbornly into the crowd. "You were probably happy I was gone."

"Ali, that's not true," Emily protested immediately, touching Ali's arm.

Ali shook her away. "Come on. It's a *little* true, isn't it?"

Spencer stared into the half inch of pink liquid left in her martini glass. It was true. After Ali disappeared, Spencer *had* been relieved to escape her taunts and tormenting. But if Ali had contacted her from the hospital, Spencer would have run the entire way to Delaware.

The three of them were quiet for a while, staring out at the masses around the bar and the DJ bopping and jerking behind the booth. A redhead climbed on a table to dance, a cadre of seven boys surrounding her like vultures. A bartender cleared a full bottle of beer from the adjacent table, and a girl with blunt-cut blond hair slipped out of the restroom. Spencer sat up straighter. Was that . . . Melissa? She squinted hard, trying to find the figure again, but she was gone. Spencer's head pounded and she felt feverish. Her eyes were obviously playing tricks on her—weren't they?

Spencer let out a long sigh. Ali stared at her, her face full of vulnerable anxiety. It was obvious how badly she wanted Spencer to forgive her. Finally, Ali crossed to the other side of the booth and flung her arms around Spencer. Spencer lightly patted Ali's back.

"*Hot,*" someone behind them whispered. They broke away and turned. Emo Super Mario was leaning against one of the columns, casually watching them over a tall glass of beer. "Can I join you?" he said in a slimy voice.

Emily let out an embarrassed titter. Ali giggled into her hand. She exchanged a naughty glance with both of them. Even Spencer knew what was coming.

"Not it!" they all cried at exactly the same time. Emily and Ali burst into hysterical laughter. Spencer laughed, too, first a bit uneasily, but then a little harder, and then harder still, until the weird, shocking tension slowly began to dissolve away.

She squeezed Ali's hand and drew her into a bear hug. Somehow, against all the odds, she had her friend—and her sister—back.

14

REVENGE IS THE NEW BLACK

At exactly 5:38 P.M. the following night, Hanna, Courtney, Kate, Naomi, and Riley emerged from the subway in front of the New York Public Library steps. A bunch of teenage tourists in platform sneakers were taking pictures of one another in front of the lion statues.

"This way," Hanna said authoritatively, turning left toward Bryant Park. Tents fluttered over the trees, reminding Hanna of white-capped waves. She wore a silk charmeuse DVF dress with an abstract floral print and a slimming waist tie. It wasn't technically in stores yet—when Sasha at Otter heard that Hanna was going to the show, she dug out her only sample and let Hanna borrow it. She was also wearing a pair of royal purple DVF platforms she bought in the fall, and she'd broken down and purchased the designer's metal-beaded slouch bag even though she was pretty sure it had maxed out her credit card.

None of the others looked nearly as good—Naomi and Kate were wearing DVF dresses from last season, and

Riley's slightly pilled wrap dress was from *two* seasons ago—
horrors. Courtney wasn't wearing anything by the designer,
opting instead for a simple Marc Jacobs wool dress and
brown ankle boots. She carried herself so confidently,
though, that Hanna wondered if it was actually the chicer
decision. What if it was gauche to wear a designer's clothes
to her fashion show, like the out-of-town dorks who wore
I.♥ NY T-shirts?

Hanna brushed the thought away. The day had been
fantastic so far. Hanna had sat with the others at lunch,
chatting excitedly about which celebrities they might
see at the show—Madonna? Taylor Momsen? Natalie
Portman? Then, they'd boarded the Amtrak Acela at
Thirtieth Street Station and spent the hour-long train
ride to New York City taking swigs of champagne from
a bottle Naomi had stolen from her dad, giggling every
time the rail-thin, stick-up-her-butt business lady sitting
next to them gave them dirty looks. Okay, so they didn't
realize they were sitting in the train's Quiet Car, which
had stricter rules than the Rosewood Day library. But
that only made it funnier.

Naomi poked Courtney's shoulder as they strode down
Fortieth Street. "We should go to that restaurant you read
about in Daily Candy, don't you think?"

"Definitely," Courtney said, ducking around a pungent-
smelling hot dog cart. "But only if Hanna wants to." She
shot Hanna a covert smile. Ever since they'd shared that
weird moment about Iris, Courtney had had Hanna's back.

They turned into the park. The place was mobbed with fashion people, each skinnier, prettier, and more glamorous than the last. In front of a big sign for Mercedes-Benz, *E!* was interviewing a woman who'd been a guest judge on *Project Runway*. A film crew was positioned right at the entrance of the DVF show, shooting every invitee who paraded into the tent.

Naomi grabbed Riley's arm. "Oh my God, we're going to be totally famous."

"Maybe we'll be in *Teen Vogue*!" Kate gushed. "Or Page Six!"

Hanna was smiling so broadly that her cheeks hurt. She waltzed up to the coordinator manning the door, an angular black man wearing pink lipstick. Cameras swiveled and focused on her face. She tried to pretend they weren't there. That was what famous actresses did when confronted with the paparazzi.

"Hi, our reservations are under Marin," Hanna said in a cool, professional voice, whipping out the five tickets she'd carefully printed out on heavy-stock paper last night. She shot Naomi and the others an excited smile, and they grinned back graciously.

The coordinator studied the invites and smirked. "Aw, how sweet. Someone knows how to use Photoshop!"

Hanna blinked. "Huh?"

He handed the invites back. "Honey, to get into this tent, you need a black key with the DVF logo on the front. One hundred people received them a month ago. These flimsy things won't get you squat."

It felt as though the guy had kicked Hanna in the spleen with his silver platform shoe. "My mom sent me these!" she wailed. "They're real!"

The guy jutted out a hip. "Mommy's got some explaining to do." He made a shooing motion with his hands. "Go on back to day care, girls."

The buildings around Bryant Park crept in closer. Sweat began to slowly snake down Hanna's forehead. The camera crew panned over Hanna's face, and someone whispered *Pretty Little Liar*. A couple of skinny girls were typing frantically on their PDAs. This would probably be splashed all over fashion blogs and Twitter feeds in minutes. They'd probably be "random fugs" on Go Fug Yourself.

Naomi yanked Hanna out of line and pushed her against a scrawny tree. "What the hell, Hanna?"

"She did this on purpose," Riley hissed nastily, sidling up behind them. "You were right, Naomi. Someone like *her* could never get tickets to this thing."

"I didn't know!" Hanna protested, her heels sinking into the slushy dirt around the tree trunk. "I'll call my mom. She can work this out."

"There's nothing *to* work out," Kate spat, her face inches from Hanna's. Her breath smelled like stale pretzels. "We gave you a chance, and you blew it."

Courtney crossed her arms, but didn't say anything.

"You're never going to be popular at Rosewood Day

again," Naomi threatened. She pulled her BlackBerry out of her clutch and grabbed Riley's arm. "Let's go to the Waverly Inn." She shot a menacing look at Hanna. "Don't you *dare* follow us."

The four of them disappeared into the crowd. Hanna turned away, staring into a nearby trash can that was filled with plastic champagne glasses. Two girls with long, shiny hair passed, each holding a black key with the DVF label stamped on the front. "I'm so psyched for the show," one of them trilled. She was wearing the same dress Hanna had on, except in a size zero instead of a four. *Bitch.*

Whipping out her cell phone, she dialed her mom's number in Singapore, not caring that it probably cost a trillion dollars to connect. The phone rang six times before her mom picked up. "I can't believe you!" Hanna howled. "You ruined my life!"

". . . *Hanna?*" Ms. Marin said, her voice sounding tinny and far away. "What's going on?"

"Why would you send me fake tickets to a fashion show?" Hanna kicked a pebble, causing a few nearby pigeons to scatter. "It's bad enough you ditched me and left me with Dad, who hates me, and Kate, who wants to ruin my life! Did you have to embarrass me in front of everyone, too?"

"*What* tickets?" Ms. Marin said.

Hanna gritted her teeth. "Tickets to the Diane von Furstenberg show in Bryant Park? The ones you e-mailed me the other day? Or are you so consumed with your job that you've already forgotten?"

"I never sent you tickets," her mother said, her voice suddenly laced with concern. "Are you sure the e-mail was from me?"

A bunch of lights in a skyscraper across the street snapped on. Pedestrians crossed from one side of Forty-second Street to the other in an amorphous herd. Goose bumps rose on Hanna's arms. If her mom hadn't sent those fake invitations, who had?

"Hanna?" Ms. Marin asked after a pause. "Honey, are you all right? Is there something we need to talk about?"

"No," Hanna said quickly, stabbing the END button. Then she staggered back to the library and sat down below one of the stone lions. There was a newspaper kiosk on the sidewalk, a copy of today's *New York Post* face out. Billy Ford's wild eyes glowered back at Hanna, his expression spellbindingly chilling, his long blond hair plastered to his sallow forehead. *Ford Didn't Do It* blared the headline.

A stiff wind gusted, blowing the top newspaper loose. It fluttered across the sidewalk, coming to a stop at a pair of familiar brown ankle boots. Hanna's gaze traveled from the boots all the way up to the heart-shaped face topped with blond hair. "Oh," she spurted, surprised.

"Hi," Courtney said, a smile on her face.

Hanna lowered her head. "What do you want?"

Courtney plopped down next to her. "Are you okay?"

Hanna didn't answer.

"They'll get over it."

"No they won't. I blew it," Hanna wailed over a grumbling Big Apple tour bus. She had a sudden craving for Cheez-Its. "I'm officially a loser."

"No you're not."

"Yes, I am." Hanna set her jaw. Maybe this was something she had to accept. "Before I met your sister, I was really lame. I don't even know why she wanted to be friends with me. I'm not cool. I've never been cool. I can't change that."

"Hanna," Courtney said sternly. "That's the stupidest thing you've ever said."

Hanna snorted. "You've known me for two days."

Headlights flashed across Courtney's face. "I've known you for a lot longer than that."

Hanna raised her head and stared at the girl on the steps. "Huh?"

Courtney cocked her head. "Come on. I thought you'd known for a while. Since the hospital."

A chilly wind kicked up, blowing around cigarette butts and spare bits of trash. "The . . . hospital?"

"Don't you remember?" Courtney smiled hopefully. "I visited you when you were in a coma."

A hazy memory of a blond figure wavered and wobbled in Hanna's mind. A girl had leaned over her bed murmuring *I'm okay, I'm okay.* But Hanna had always thought that girl was . . .

Hanna blinked in disbelief. "*Ali?*"

The girl next to her nodded. She extended her arms out *ta-daa!* style.

"What?" Hanna's heart thundered. "*How?*"

Ali told her story. Hanna gasped at the end of almost every sentence, barely believing her ears. She gazed at the pedestrians walking down Fifth Avenue. A woman pushed a Silver Cross baby carriage, yakking on a Motorola Droid. A gay couple in matching John Varvatos leather jackets walked their French bulldog. It was amazing that their mundane lives could proceed apace amidst such a life-altering revelation.

She took Hanna's hands. "Hanna, I never thought you were a loser. And seriously, *look* at you now." She leaned back and gestured to Hanna's hair and outfit. "You're stunning."

The surface of Hanna's skin throbbed. In sixth grade, she'd felt like the Michelin Tire Man next to Ali. Her stomach bulged and her braces made her cheeks puffy. Ali had always looked so flawless—whether she was in her field hockey skirt or the white dress she'd worn to seventh-grade graduation. For years Hanna had longed to show Ali her makeover, to prove that she was fabulous, too. "Thanks," she whispered, feeling thoroughly disembodied, as if caught in a dream.

"You and I are the ones who deserve to be popular, Hanna." Ali's eyes hardened for such a brief moment that Hanna wondered if she'd imagined it. "Not your stepsister.

And *especially* not Naomi or Riley. So you know what we need to do?"

"W-what?" Hanna stuttered.

A coy smile slunk onto Ali's face. All of a sudden, she was pure Ali again—irresistible, intoxicating, and utterly in control of everything. She stepped off the stairs and extended her arm for a cab. One pulled up immediately. Ali climbed in and motioned for Hanna to follow.

"Penn Station," Ali said to the driver, slamming the door. Then she turned back to Hanna. "We ditch the bitches," she said. "And then we take them down."

15

WHEN YOU WISH UPON A WELL

Late Thursday night, Aria stood in her bedroom at Byron's new house, examining the fringed red dress she'd bought for the Valentine's Day dance. Would Noel think it was artistic and stylish . . . or kooky?

Suddenly, a flicker outside the big bedroom window caught her eye. A figure jogged past the house, her lithe body illuminated by the amber-hued streetlight. Aria immediately recognized the pink Windbreaker, black running tights, and dirty blond hair tucked into a silver beanie. Spencer's sister, Melissa, religiously ran the neighborhood roads every afternoon.

But never at *night.* Aria's heart started to pound as she remembered Melissa lurking outside Courtney's house yesterday. An eerie feeling crept into her bones. Aria pulled on a sweatshirt, rammed her feet into her Uggs, and went outside.

The night was frigid and still. A fat, bloated moon hung in the sky. The houses loomed huge and imposing, and most people's porch lights were already off for the night. The air still had a faint odor of charred earth to it from the fire, and Aria could make out jagged tree stumps in the woods. She spied the reflective tape on Melissa's sneakers at the end of the street and started to run, following her at a safe distance.

Melissa passed the big Dutch Colonial whose owners rotated colorful porch flags with the seasons, the massive stone farmhouse with the man-made pond in the backyard, and then the big Victorian with the memorial at the curb. *We'll miss you, Ian,* someone had spelled out with marigolds. Now that everyone presumed that Ian was innocent—and dead—the town had set up a series of wreaths, lacrosse sticks, and old Rosewood Day soccer jerseys on the Thomases' muddy lawn in his memory.

Melissa circled the cul-de-sac and disappeared down a path toward the woods. Aria stealthily followed, growing nervous. Technically, people weren't allowed back here—the cops were still hunting for Ian's body.

Taking a deep breath, Aria pushed through the brambles to follow her. Twigs snapped and crackled. The air was thick with putrid smoke. Melissa's bobbing sneakers disappeared up a steep rise. Aria's lungs filled and emptied, rushing to keep up. She was so far into the woods now that she could barely see the lights from the houses. The only thing she could make out was Spencer's family's dilapidated barn, way off through the trees.

A pair of eyes blinked at her from a high tree branch.

Something scuttled on the forest floor. Aria gasped but kept going. She staggered up the hill on all fours, panting hard. But when she reached the top, she didn't see Melissa anywhere. It was as if she had evaporated into thin air.

"Aria?"

Aria screamed and whirled around. A face swam into view. First Aria saw her heart-shaped jaw, then her glistening blue eyes, and then her bloodred Cheshire cat smile.

"C-Courtney?" she stammered.

"I didn't realize anyone else knew about this place," Courtney said, tucking a stray lock of blond hair under her maroon wool hat.

Aria ran her hands over her bumpy ponytail. Her heart thrummed in her ears. "D-did you see Spencer's sister? Melissa? I followed her here."

Courtney shook her head, looking confused. "It's just me and the moon."

Aria shivered, her lungs burning from the cold. She wanted out of here, *now*, but her limbs wouldn't move. "W-what are *you* doing here?"

"Just checking out an old haunt," Courtney said. She leaned against a crumbling structure Aria had never seen before. It looked like a round brick base, overgrown with moss. Half of an A-shaped post still existed, the wood brittle and rotted. A rusty metal bucket lay in the grass nearby.

Aria put her hand to her mouth, slowly filling in the

missing pieces. It was a *wishing well.* Just like the one Ali had drawn on her Time Capsule flag. Her limbs began to shake.

"I used to come here to think." Courtney perched on the edge of the stone, letting her feet dangle into the well. "It was the only place that was just mine. It's why I drew it on my Time Capsule flag."

Aria's mouth dropped open. *Her* Time Capsule flag? "Excuse me?"

An owl hooted. A cloud shaped like a hand floated over the moon. Courtney threw a clump of frozen moss down the well. Aria didn't hear it hit the bottom. "I know Jason gave you the flag." She turned to look at Aria. "I'm glad you had it."

Aria blinked fast. "W-what the hell is going on?"

Courtney raised her hands in surrender. "Don't freak out." Her voice made a little puff of smoke in the air. "But I'm not Courtney. I'm Ali."

Aria's knees buckled. She scrambled backward, slipping on some wet leaves.

"Please don't run away," Courtney pleaded. The moon illuminated the whites of her eyes and her ultra-bleached teeth, like a human jack-o'-lantern. "Just let me explain."

Aria didn't move as Courtney—or whoever she was—quickly summarized the truth about her sister, the murder, and the switch. "Hanna, Spencer, and Emily all know already," she concluded. "I knew you'd be the hardest to tell. All that stuff with your dad . . ." She jumped off the well and approached Aria. She tentatively put a cashmere-gloved hand on Aria's shoulder. "I was awful to you. But I've changed. I want us to be friends again, just like we used to be when we first got together in sixth grade. Remember how awesome it was?"

Aria's lips felt paralyzed. Was this *Ali* standing in front of her? It *could* be possible. Something had been so strange about Courtney from the beginning—she'd known more about Aria and Rosewood than she should have.

Ali stood there, her eyes wide, pleading. "Just think about it, okay? Try to see things from my perspective."

Aria felt a longing twinge, wanting things to be the way they once were back when they'd first become friends. Things *had* been awesome for a while: They'd taken tons of trips to the Poconos, spent hours at one another's houses, made silly movies with Aria's video camera. For once, Aria hadn't been a kooky loner but part of a group.

And then Ali pivoted and walked away. Her footsteps crunched loudly for a few moments before fading into the distance.

Aria started back down the hill toward her house. *I want us to be friends again. Just think about it, okay?* Part of her wanted to tell Ali that bygones were bygones. She wanted a best friend again. But something was holding her back. Could Aria really believe that Ali was sorry for everything she'd done and had changed her ways? She'd been back for only a few days, and she already was telling lies again, pretending she'd never been to Rosewood Day or seen Noel Kahn's house before. She'd put on a pretty convincing act, blubbering about how devastated she was about her father's affair. Was it really just to get Aria to open up about her own family dysfunction all over again?

Aria breathed out, the smell of rust and something vaguely pondlike filling her nostrils. Then she noticed something white at her feet and stopped. Something was buried deep in the dirt in the side of the hill.

After a moment's hesitation, Aria crouched down and pulled at it. Chunks of soil and dead leaves cascaded to the ground as she wrenched it free. It was a tattered envelope. Had the backhoes dredged it up when removing some of the old tree stumps?

She tore the envelope open and plunged her hand inside. Her fingers touched something with hard, square edges. Taking a deep breath, she pulled out two blurry Polaroids. Aria furrowed her brow, her hands mottled purple from the cold. The first was a photo of four girls sitting in a circle on a round rug, their heads down. Candles flickered around them. A fifth girl with long blond hair and a heart-shaped face stood, her arms in the air, her eyes closed.

Aria's heart started to pound. This looked like one of the Polaroids Billy had taken of their end-of-seventh-grade sleepover.

She examined the second Polaroid. The flash had made a hot yellow circle at the top of the frame. Aria felt wobbly on her feet, and her teeth chattered. Somehow, maybe because of the angle of the camera or the refractive light from the flash, this picture showed not what was happening inside . . . but outside. There was a ghostly reflection in the window showing a pair of hands and a shadowy, ghoulish face. Whoever it was had blond hair like Billy's, but the features were softer, more feminine. The image was blurry, but the person's nose was small and straight, and the eyes were round and rimmed with dark lashes.

Aria could barely breathe. She stared at the reflection until her eyes burned. As much as she wanted to believe that the person in the window looked like Billy, she knew it wasn't true.

Which meant that someone else had been watching them that night.

16

IF NOT NOW, EM, WHEN?

The following morning, Emily and her sister Carolyn walked into the Rosewood Diner. Their grueling swimming practice had ended a little early, which meant they actually had time to eat a real meal before school.

The diner's owners left their Christmas lights up all year long, which made the room feel cozy and festive. The kitchen smelled of pancakes, syrup, sausages, and coffee. A couple of discarded newspapers lay on the counter. *Photo in Window Isn't of Ford* read one of the headlines. Beneath it was a scan of the blurry Polaroid Aria had told Emily about. She'd called late last night, explaining that she'd found two photos in the woods. She'd dropped off the photos anonymously, not wanting to draw any more attention to herself.

Emily stared hard at the fuzzy image. The face was overexposed from the flash, making it look like an apparition. The person had blond hair like Billy's, but the shapes of the person's jaw, eyes, and nose were completely different. The space behind Emily's eyes started to throb. Why did Billy have those Polaroids if he wasn't the one who'd taken the pictures? Did he have an accomplice that night? Or had someone planted them in his car?

Emily followed Carolyn into the big red booth. Her cell phone beeped from inside her swim bag. *One new text.* It was from Courtney DiLaurentis. *Ali.*

Can't wait to see you in gym 2day. XX

Emily's heart flipped. *Can't wait to see you too,* she texted back, watching the little envelope spin until the text was sent.

She could still taste Ali's minty breath and feel her soft, full lips on hers. She could still see Ali dancing seductively at that club on Wednesday night, the spotlight shining on the crown of her golden head.

Carolyn leaned over and glanced at Emily's cell phone screen. Her eyes widened. "Are you and Courtney friends?"

"She seems nice," Emily said, trying not to give anything away.

Carolyn folded the menu and slid it to the edge of the table. "It's so weird that Ali had a twin. Did you ever suspect?"

Emily shrugged. In hindsight, it all fit together. She should've guessed something weird was going on the day before the seventh-grade sleepover. When Ali had met the girls on the porch, she'd had no memory of talking to them in her room just moments before. Then later that same afternoon, Emily had excused herself to use the DiLaurentises' bathroom. Inside, she'd heard Jason whispering angrily to someone on the stairs. "You'd better stop it," he warned. "You know how that pisses them off."

"I'm not hurting anyone," another voice had protested. It sounded a lot like *Ali*, but it had clearly been Courtney. Jason was probably scolding her for impersonating her sister—again.

She tried to drown me, Ali had said. *She wanted to kill me to* be *me.* Emily shuddered.

But what about the other time Courtney had been home, when she'd switched from the Radley to the Preserve? Ali had said it was early in sixth grade. Could it have been the same Saturday that Emily, Spencer, and the others had sneaked into Ali's yard, hoping to steal her Time Capsule flag? Emily remembered hearing an argument from inside the DiLaurentises' house—Ali had screamed "Stop it!" and then someone had yelled "Stop it!" back in the same high-pitched voice. She'd figured it was Jason, but it also could have been Courtney.

That was the first day Ali had ever talked to any of them, and for a while, she'd seemed almost *friendly*. She didn't even stop the conversation when Mrs. DiLaurentis stepped out on the porch and told Ali she was leaving.

Looking back on it now, Emily wondered if Ali's family was taking Courtney to the Preserve, the new facility. If she'd paid more attention to the DiLaurentises' Mercedes as it pulled away from the house, would she have seen a face eerily identical to Ali's in the backseat?

The waitress approached their table and asked if they'd decided what they wanted for breakfast. Carolyn ordered a western omelet, and Emily requested a Belgian waffle. After the waitress strode away, Carolyn dumped a container of creamer into her coffee mug. "Courtney seems really different than Ali."

Emily stirred her hot chocolate, trying to remain neutral. "Why do you say that?"

"I'm not sure. I can't really put my finger on it, but the differences are there."

The bell on the counter rang. The waitress carried two trays of food in her arms, teetering slightly beneath the weight. Emily wished she could tell Carolyn the truth about Ali, but Ali had sworn her to secrecy. Emily wondered just how long Ali would have to pretend to be Courtney. Until she was eighteen? Forever?

Carolyn raised an eyebrow, looking past Emily at something out the window. "Isn't that Officer Wilden?"

Emily turned. Two people were huddled together across the parking lot. A blond girl in a checkered coat was talking to a familiar cop. It was Wilden and Spencer's sister, Melissa. Whatever they were saying looked heated.

Melissa shook her finger in Wilden's face. Wilden said something back, waving his hand like he didn't believe what Melissa was saying. Melissa threw her hands in the air in apparent frustration, and Wilden walked away. She called out to him, but he didn't turn around.

"Whoa," Carolyn said quietly. "What was *that* all about?"

"No clue," Emily said softly.

The door of the diner opened, and two guys in Tate Prep Diving warm-up jackets strutted in. Carolyn turned back to Emily, taking another sip of coffee. "So are you and Isaac going to the Valentine's Day dance? I haven't seen him around lately."

Isaac. For a moment, Emily couldn't even remember her old boyfriend's face. Not long ago, she'd thought Isaac Colbert was the love of her life—enough even to sleep with him. But then he hadn't believed Emily when she told him that his mother was tormenting her. It felt like it had happened a millennium ago. "Uh . . . I doubt it."

"What happened?"

Emily pretended to be fascinated by the laminated place mat in front of her, a kitschy, fact-filled map of the United States. Her parents and sister still thought she'd gone on a choir trip to Boston with Isaac a few weeks ago, but she'd really been in Amish Country, unearthing information on Wilden's past. When the cops brought Emily home the night she'd almost broken into the Rosewood PD evidence room—the same night Jenna was killed—she'd told her mom she was dressed in Amish garb for a role-playing game she'd taken part in during the Boston trip. Emily was pretty sure her mom didn't believe her, but Mrs. Fields hadn't pressed the issue.

After a couple of seconds of Emily not answering, Carolyn shifted her weight, a smile crawling across her face. "You're not with Isaac anymore, are you?"

"No," Emily admitted, choosing her words carefully. "I like someone else."

Carolyn's eyes widened. It probably wasn't hard for her to guess who: Mona-as-A had made Emily's longtime crush on Ali very plain to the entire school.

"Is Courtney . . . *like* that?" Carolyn whispered.

"I don't know." Emily pressed her thumb into the tines of the fork. *I always wanted to do that again,* Ali had said. *Was* Ali like that? Why else would she say those things?

The waitress set down their plates. Emily stared at her syrup-and-butter-laden waffle. She was suddenly too nervous to be hungry.

Carolyn placed her palms flat on the table. "You should ask her to the dance," she decided.

"I can't!" Emily exclaimed, a little surprised that her sister was being so open-minded.

"Why not? What do you have to lose?" Carolyn popped a bite of omelet into her mouth. "You can ride with me and Topher. We're renting a limo." Topher was Carolyn's longtime boyfriend.

Emily opened her mouth, and then shut it again.

Carolyn didn't understand. This wasn't a normal crush like the one she had on Maya or Isaac. For years she'd thought of being with Ali, of going to Stanford with her and then maybe—if she was lucky—getting a little house together with one of those cute rooster weather vanes out front. The idea of coming on too strong and ruining her chances with Ali paralyzed Emily. Ali's opinion meant everything, and if Ali rejected her, Emily wasn't sure what she'd do. There was no risk in getting crushed if she kept her feelings to herself.

Emily's phone buzzed again, and she yanked it open. Ali had texted back with a line of *X*s. Then again, what if Ali wanted this, too?

17

WHO'S AFRAID OF THE BAD, BIG SISTER?

Around the same time that morning, Spencer climbed into Melissa's idling SUV and waited as her sister ran inside to get her sunglasses. In a rare show of helpfulness, Melissa had offered to drive Spencer to school. Spencer dropped her Kate Spade tote on the backseat. The car smelled overpoweringly of cinnamon gum, and the radio blared. "After a message from our sponsors, we'll discuss the photographs that shed new light on the Rosewood Serial Killer case," a reporter announced.

The broadcast cut to a commercial for Treasures in the Attic, a local antique shop, and Spencer snapped the radio off. She'd received a text from Aria this morning about the photos she'd found in the woods, but Spencer hadn't seen them yet. All she knew was that the photographer might be a girl. Spencer had been doing her best to ignore the inconsistencies in the case against Billy, but now . . .

An icy hand curled over Spencer's hand and she jumped. "Earth to Spencer," Melissa chirped, slamming the door. "Are you in there?"

"Sorry," Spencer said as Melissa pulled out of the driveway and almost backed into the Jenna shrine. It had grown to three times its original size. The Ali shrine at the base of the DiLaurentises' old curb was going strong, too, full of candles, flowers, stuffed bears, and old photos of Ali as a kid.

If only people really knew, Spencer thought. The girl in those old photos was still alive. It was so hard to believe.

Melissa was eyeing the Ali shrine, too. "Has Courtney seen that?" she asked.

Spencer's stomach swooped. It was strange to hear the name *Courtney* now that she knew the truth. "I don't know."

At the end of the street, Mrs. Sullivan, who lived on the corner, was out walking her two Shetland sheepdogs. Melissa turned out of their neighborhood, and they drove in silence for a few minutes, sweeping past Johnson Farm, which sold organic butter and veggies, and then the big township park. A couple of people were jogging, their heads down and braced against the wind.

Melissa pushed her aviators to the top of her head and glanced at Spencer out of the corner of her eye. "Have you hung out with Courtney at all?"

"Uh-huh," Spencer answered, pulling the sleeves of her coat over her bare hands.

Melissa tightened her grip on the steering wheel. "Are you sure that's a good idea?"

They paused at a stop sign. A squirrel darted across the road, its bushy tail high in the air. "Why wouldn't it be?" Spencer asked.

Melissa tapped her left foot on the floor. "You don't know much about her. When Jason told me about her, he said she was really unstable."

Then she hit the gas again, jolting across the intersection. Spencer wished she could tell Melissa exactly what she *didn't* know—that the unstable sister was dead. "You've never even spoken to her," she said instead.

Melissa's voice hardened. "I just think you should be careful with her. Don't jump into a friendship too fast."

They pulled up the drive of Rosewood Day and came to a stop behind a bunch of yellow school buses. Kids trudged down the bus steps and ran to the double doors, eager to escape the biting cold. Spencer pointed at her sister accusingly. "You're just saying that because you hated Ali and you don't like Courtney by extension."

Melissa rolled her eyes. "Don't be a drama queen. I just don't want you to get hurt."

"Sure you don't," Spencer growled. "Because *you've* certainly never tried to hurt me." She jerked the door open, climbed out, and then slammed it behind her.

The halls smelled like freshly baked pastries from Steam. As Spencer approached her locker, Ali emerged from the bathroom. Her blue eyes twinkled, perfectly matching her school blazer. "Hey!" she cried, wrapping an arm around Spencer's shoulders. "Just the person I wanted to see. We're going to get ready for the dance tomorrow together, right?"

"Yeah," Spencer said, spinning the combination dial of her locker too fast and missing one of the numbers. Frustrated, she kicked the metal door.

Ali frowned. "Is something wrong?"

Spencer rolled her head around her neck, trying to settle down. "Melissa is driving me crazy."

Ali put her hands on her hips. A couple of guys on the soccer team passed, giving her appreciative whistles. "Did you have another fight about your mom?"

"No . . ." Spencer finally got her locker open. She shrugged out of her coat and jammed it on the hook. "Actually, it was about you."

"Me?" Ali pressed her palm to her chest.

"Yeah." Spencer barked out a laugh. "I told her we were hanging out. She said I should stay away from you."

Ali picked at an invisible imperfection on her blazer. "Well, maybe she's looking out for you."

Spencer sniffed. "You *know* Melissa. She definitely *wasn't* looking out for me."

A muscle in Ali's neck tensed. "So why did she say it?"

Spencer chewed on her bottom lip. Melissa and Ali had never gotten along. Ali was the only one who hadn't sucked up to Melissa back then. Right before she'd disappeared, Ali had even teased Melissa that Ian might get a new girlfriend while Melissa was on vacation in Prague. And Melissa had *definitely* suspected that Ali was fooling around with Ian. A couple of months ago, Spencer and Melissa were in the family's hot tub in the backyard, and Melissa said she'd known that Ian had cheated on her in high school. "Ian is going to regret it for the rest of his life," she'd said. Spencer asked what she was going to do to the girl he'd cheated with, and Melissa smiled deviously. "Who says I haven't done something to her already?"

A locker slammed close by. Someone's cell phone tinkled. The between-classes music halted, a clear indication that they had to get to homeroom. Spencer glanced up at Ali, who was staring at her, probably wondering what she was thinking. "Do you think there's any way Melissa could know you aren't Courtney?" she asked.

Ali backed up. Her forehead wrinkled. "No. No way."

"Are you *sure*?"

"I'm positive." Ali brushed her long blond hair over her shoulder. A freshman boy nearby double-taked and dropped his biology textbook on the marble floor. "Honestly, Spence? Melissa's probably just jealous. You both have another sister now . . . and I like *you* better."

A warm, comforting feeling seeped into Spencer's bones as Ali said her good-byes and headed down the art wing. Spencer cut through the lobby toward homeroom, but when she passed Steam, a rack of today's

Philadelphia Sentinel made her stop short. "Oh my God," she whispered.

The Polaroid Aria had found last night was splashed on the front page, the blurry, spooky eyes gazing straight at Spencer. Spencer recognized the face immediately.

Melissa.

18

TWO FASHIONISTAS, ONE CUNNING PLAN

Even though it was barely four o' clock on Friday, Rive Gauche, the French bistro in the King James Mall, was teeming with well-dressed, well-groomed prep school girls. Gorgeous leather purses were slung over empty seats, and large, glossy shopping bags embossed with luxe designer labels were tucked under tables. Waiters dressed in crisp white shirts and skinny black pants swirled around the diners, delivering bottles of wine and crèmes brûlées. The air smelled like clarified-butter-drenched escargot and wonderfully greasy Belgian fries.

Hanna sighed with pleasure. She hadn't been to Rive Gauche in a while, and she'd missed it. Merely standing in the lobby of Rive Gauche gave her an extreme sense of well-being. It was like instant therapy.

The hostess led Hanna and Ali through the dining room. Both girls toted heavy bags from Otter. They'd spent the past hour and a half trying on almost everything in the store. For once, it wasn't all about Ali twirling in front of the three-way mirrors in size-two dresses and twenty-five-inch-waist skinny jeans while Hanna slumped on the couch like an ugly, pimply manatee. Today, Hanna looked just as beautiful in high-waist trousers, wrap dresses, and slinky shifts. Ali had even asked Hanna for some fashion advice on light denim—she *had* been locked up in a hospital for three years, after all, and was out of touch.

The only teensy annoyance was when Hanna remembered the last time she'd been in Otter's dressing room with a friend—Mike had taken Hanna there on her first date, and he'd picked out all kinds of skanky, way-too-tight outfits for her to try on. She'd mentioned Mike briefly to Ali, asking if Naomi and Riley were behind the Skidz thing. Ali said she didn't know for sure, but it wouldn't surprise her.

Ali and Hanna plopped down in a booth. Ali pulled a silk scarf out of her Otter bag and wound it around her neck. "I want everyone to come to the Poconos house tomorrow after the Valentine's dance. We can get drunk, go in the hot tub, reconnect. . . ."

"That would be awesome." Hanna clapped.

Ali looked uncertain for a moment. "Do you think the others will go for it?"

"Spencer and Emily definitely will," Hanna answered. Aria, on the other hand, wouldn't stop talking about some old wishing well. "Ali said it was the inspiration for the well on her flag," she'd whispered urgently to Hanna last night on the phone. "Did she ever tell *you* about a well?"

"No, but who cares?" Hanna had answered, not understanding where Aria was going with this. So Ali had a secret wishing well she kept all to herself. Who cared?

"We'll have to pick up alcohol and snacks," Ali said, ticking the items off on her fingers.

Hanna imagined a trip to the Poconos. They'd play drinking games and tell secrets. They'd climb into the hot tub, clad in string bikinis, except this time Hanna wouldn't self-consciously cover her chubby stomach. Back in the day, Hanna had been plagued by the worry that she was the joke of the group, the girl who was always on the verge of being ousted. But there was a new Hanna in town—a pretty, skinny, *confident* Hanna.

A skinny waitress with a French twist and high cheekbones flitted to their table. Hanna handed back the menu without looking at it. "We'll get *moules frites*."

The waitress nodded and left, pausing to check on a table of Quaker schoolgirls by the window.

Ali whipped out her iPhone from its cracked leather case. "Okay. On to Operation TTBD—Take Those Bitches Down."

"Great," Hanna chirped. She was so ready. Kate, Naomi, and Riley had strutted around school today, telling everyone that all Hanna's couture was as fake as the DVF fashion show tickets. And that morning at breakfast, Kate had complained to Hanna's father that Hanna had dragged her all the way to New York as a joke, making her miss the *Hamlet* rehearsal. As usual, Hanna's dad believed Kate. Hanna didn't even bother to defend herself. What was the point?

"I've figured out the perfect thing to do." Ali tapped her iPhone's screen. "So at the sleepover the other day?"

"Yeah." Hanna shoved her Otter carrier bags under the booth.

Ali started pressing buttons on the phone. "Well, before you got home, we were buzzed on rum, and they all wrote love letters to their crushes."

"Love letters? Really?" Hanna wrinkled her nose. "That's so . . ."

"Seventh grade?" Ali rolled her eyes. "I know. Anyway, you should've seen the letters they wrote. Really juicy stuff." She leaned across the table, her mouth so close that Hanna could smell her strawberry lip gloss. "I stayed out of it, of course, because as *Courtney*, I haven't been here long enough to have a crush on anyone yet. But right before I left, I stole the letters and scanned them on the machine in your mom's old office. They're all on my phone. We can print them and pass them out at the dance. Valentine's Day is all about unrequited love, after all!"

Ali brought up the images on her phone and waved the screen in Hanna's face. Kate's letter gushed about how she had a secret crush on Sean Ackard, Hanna's ex, vowing to attend V Club sessions with him. Riley's love letter was to Seth Cardiff, a stocky swimmer. Apparently she loved how he looked in his tight Speedo. Naomi's letter was to Christophe Briggs, the flaming senior director of the Rosewood Day drama club, saying she wanted a crack at "turning him straight." Each girl had signed their love letter with a red-lipstick kiss. They must have been wasted when they wrote them.

Humiliating.

"Sweet." Hanna high-fived Ali.

"So until the dance, I need to pretend Naomi, Riley, Kate, and I are still BFFs. They can't know we're talking, otherwise it'll blow the whole thing."

"Of course," Hanna agreed. It would be such an appropriate, satisfying repeat of the *first* time Ali ditched Naomi and Riley, just before the Rosewood Day Charity Drive in sixth grade. Hanna would never forget the mortified looks on Naomi's and Riley's faces when they'd realized they'd been replaced. *So* satisfying.

"Why did you ditch Naomi and Riley back in seventh grade anyway?" Hanna asked. It was something she and Ali had never discussed—Hanna had been too afraid to bring it up, worried that it might jinx her friendship with Ali. But that was years ago, and they were finally equals.

The double doors to the kitchen swished open, and a waitress emerged carrying a tray of dishes. A muscle near Ali's mouth twitched. "I realized they weren't really my friends after all."

"Did they do something to you?" Hanna pressed.

"You could say that," Ali mumbled vaguely.

A group of girls a few tables over flipped through a copy of *Us Weekly*, gossiping about a starlet's botched plastic surgery. An old married couple shared a piece of molten chocolate cake. A steaming plate of mussels and fries appeared in front of Hanna and Ali. Ali dove in right away, but Hanna hung back for a moment, trying to figure out what Naomi and Riley had done.

"The letter thing is an awesome plan." Hanna grabbed a fry from the top of the pile. "It'll be like the famous Will Butterfield note!"

Ali paused, a shiny mussel shell between her thumb and forefinger. There was a wrinkle between her eyebrows. "Huh?"

"You know," Hanna encouraged. "The time you found that note Will Butterfield wrote to his math teacher and got Spencer to read it over the morning announcements? It was classic."

The haze slowly dissolved from Ali's eyes and her lips curved up. "Oh. Yeah. Right." Her smile quickly wobbled into a frown. "Sorry. It just seems so long ago."

Hanna popped a mussel into her mouth, wondering if she shouldn't have brought it up.

"It's cool," Hanna said, patting Ali's arm. But Ali's attention was elsewhere. Hanna followed her gaze to the mall atrium. Someone was crouched behind the burbling fountain, staring at them. Hanna's stomach seized. There was a flash of blond hair and Hanna thought about the

Polaroids Aria had found. That face in the window. Now
the news was saying that Billy might not be guilty of any
of the murders. It was like a nightmare coming true.

Hanna sneaked a peek at Ali. "Who is that?"

"I don't know," Ali whispered back. Her hands
quivered.

Hanna held her breath, watching, waiting, but then
a group of kids passed, blocking her view. By the time
they'd bounded into Banana Republic, whoever had been
watching was gone.

19

THE BIGGEST QUESTION OF EMILY'S LIFE

Sheets of cold rain pounded on the roof of Emily's Volvo wagon as she turned into Ali's new neighborhood. The development's duck pond, with its quaint wooden gazebo and rickety footbridge, was silent and still in the cold, wintry darkness. Emily had already envisioned sitting with Ali by the duck pond's edge in the springtime, holding hands and blowing dandelion seeds across the grass. She'd imagined riding bikes with Ali around the winding streets of the development and camping out in her big backyard, waking up every few hours to kiss. And she'd pictured pulling up to Ali's house tomorrow to pick up Ali for the Valentine's Day dance, Ali descending the staircase dressed in a gorgeous red silk gown and red satin heels.

Hopefully she wasn't getting ahead of herself.

After her conversation with Carolyn at the diner, Emily had decided to ask Ali to the dance today at school. Problem was, she hadn't seen Ali anywhere. She wasn't at

Steam with Naomi, Riley, and Hanna's stepsister-to-be, Kate. Emily didn't pass her in the hallways between third and fourth period on her way to chemistry. She hadn't shown up at gym, either. During sixth period, jittery to the point of feeling sick, Emily asked for a hall pass from her ceramics teacher and roamed the school, peeking into various classrooms, hoping for a glimpse of Ali's face. The dance was the next day. She was running out of time.

The DiLaurentises' porch light was on, and the family's BMW was in the driveway. Emily took a few deep breaths, staring at the traffic light beyond Ali's street. *If it turns green in the next five seconds, Ali will say yes,* she said to herself. She slowly counted to five. The light glowed red. *Best two out of three,* she decided.

Five more seconds passed, and the traffic light was still red. Sighing, she got out of the car, strode up the walk, and rang the bell. There were footsteps, and then the door swung open. Jason DiLaurentis stood on the other side, his blond hair combed flat against his head and his face unshaven, wearing ratty jeans and a Penn T-shirt. When he saw it was Emily, his eyebrows knitted together. The last time Emily had seen Jason, he'd chewed her out for allegedly denting his car. The heated look on his face made her think he hadn't forgotten.

"Hey," Emily said, trembling slightly. "I'm here to see . . . Courtney." She caught herself just before she said *Ali.*

"Uh, sure." Jason yelled Courtney's name up the stairs, then turned back and gave Emily a long, unapologetic look. Emily's cheeks burned. She fiddled anxiously with a wooden dog statue that was sitting on the console table just for something to do with her hands.

"So you and Courtney are friends now?" Jason asked finally. "Just like that?"

"Yeah." *So?* she wanted to add.

"Hey!" Ali bounded down the stairs. Her blond hair was in a ponytail, and she was wearing a sky blue T-shirt, a color she'd always worn back in seventh grade because it drew out her eyes. "What a nice surprise!"

Emily turned back to Jason, but he'd disappeared. "Hi," she answered, feeling dizzy.

"Let's go to the den," Ali suggested, whirling around and disappearing into a room off the hall. The room was big, square, and dark, and smelled like a woodstove. A flat-screen TV was shoved against the corner, heavy velvet curtains were pulled across the windows, and a striped candy dish full of pink M&M's sat in the middle of the coffee table. A bunch of photos lay on the floor, propped up against the chairs and bookcases.

Emily leaned down to look at the photo on top of the pile. It was a picture of the DiLaurentis parents and children—only *two* children, not three. Ali was in seventh grade, her face slightly rounder, her hair a little lighter. Jason stood next to her, his mouth smiling but his eyes serious. The DiLaurentis parents rested their hands on their kids' shoulders, grinning proudly as if they had nothing to hide.

She stared again at Jason's image, still shaky from their interaction in the hall. "Are you sure your brother doesn't know who you really are?" she whispered.

Ali slumped down on the couch and shook her head vehemently. "No." She shot Emily a warning look. "And please don't tell him. My family has to believe I'm Courtney. It's the only way they'll think I'm better."

Emily leaned back, the leather making a squeaky noise under her legs. "I promise."

Then she reached out and touched Ali's hand. It was cold and a little clammy. "I missed you today. There was something I wanted to ask you."

Ali stared at Emily's hand on hers. Her lips parted slightly. "What?"

Emily's heart thumped. "Well, there's a school Valentine's Day dance tomorrow."

Ali moved her jaw. Her bottom teeth stuck out slightly.

"Anyway, I was wondering if you'd . . ." Emily paused, the words catching in her throat. "If you'd want to go with me. Like as a date. We could double with my sister and her boyfriend. It'll be really fun."

Ali pulled her hand away. "Em . . ." she started. The corners of her lips shook, as if she was suppressing a laugh.

Emily's stomach plummeted. All at once, she was transported to Ali's tree house, moments after she'd leaned over and kissed Ali's lips. Ali kissed back for a delicious few moments before she'd pulled away. "Now I know why you get so quiet when we change during gym class," she'd teased.

Emily jumped up, bumping into the corner of an enormous marble chessboard on the coffee table. The white queen wobbled, then tipped over. "I have to go."

Ali's face fell. "What? Why?"

Emily fumbled for her jacket over the back of the chair. "I just remembered. I have homework."

Ali's eyes were round and troubled. "I don't want you to leave."

Emily's chin wobbled. *Don't cry,* she told herself.

"I meant what I said the other day about how I feel about you." Ali grabbed Emily's hand. Outside, the neighbor's porch light flickered on. "But I have to get my life together first, okay?"

Emily searched for the car keys in her coat pocket. It was probably an excuse. Ali would be making fun of her for it by tomorrow. Emily shouldn't have trusted her so quickly. She clearly *hadn't* changed that much.

"I'm not going to ditch you," Ali promised, like she could tell what was galloping through Emily's mind. "The most important thing is that we're friends again. We can still hang out at the dance. And I want all of us to get ready together."

"All of us?" Emily blinked.

"You, me, Spencer, Hanna . . . " Ali looked hopeful. "Maybe even Aria? I was thinking that we could go to my family's Poconos house afterward." She squeezed Emily's hands. "I want us all to be back together again, like things used to be."

Emily sniffed, but she put her keys away.

Ali patted the cushion beside her. "*Please* stay. We need to talk about the dance, now that I know you're going. I bet you haven't even picked out a dress yet."

"Well, no. I was thinking of wearing something of my sister's."

Ali punched her playfully. "Just like old times."

Emily sat back down. It felt like her emotions had been on a high-spin cycle, but as Ali opened a copy of *Teen Vogue* and pointed out a series of party dresses that would complement Emily's peaches-and-cream complexion, her mood began to thaw. Perhaps she was losing sight of things. Ali had returned—everything else would come in time.

Ali was reaching for *Seventeen* when Emily heard footsteps in the hall. Jason stood at the foot of the stairs, glaring into the den. His forehead was wrinkled, the corners of his mouth turned sharply down, and he was gripping the banister so tightly that his knuckles were white.

Emily's mouth dropped open. But just as she was about to nudge Ali, Jason stormed out of the house, slamming the door behind him.

20

IT'S ALL ABOUT LETTING GO

Early Saturday afternoon, Aria climbed out of the Subaru, locked up, and started across the mall parking lot. Mike walked alongside her, the hood on his jacket pulled tight around his head. Aria had volunteered to escort Mike to the optician in the King James Mall to pick up a spare pair of contacts—he was constantly ripping them, but wouldn't *dare* wear his glasses. Lately, Meredith had been maniacally humming songs from *Cinderella* while decorating the baby's room—in neutral yellows, as Meredith and Byron didn't want to know the sex until the baby was born—and Aria was desperate for an excuse to get out of the house.

Aria's phone started to bleat. She pulled it out of her pocket and looked at the screen. *Wilden.* A dart of fear streaked through her stomach. Why was he calling her? Could he know she'd been the one who'd sent the police that extra photo she'd found in the woods? She hit silent and dropped the phone into her pocket again, her heart thudding hard.

She knew she'd done the right thing by giving the photos to the Rosewood PD anonymously. It was an act of self-preservation—Aria didn't want to be at the center of this case anymore. She'd considered telling the cops about seeing Melissa running into the woods, but what if it all was a big coincidence? And she *definitely* didn't want to tell the police about seeing Courtney—Ali—at the wishing well . . . or what they talked about.

"So are you going to the dance tonight?" Aria asked Mike as they trudged to the Saks entrance of the mall.

Mike glanced at her out of the corner of his eye. "What do *you* think?"

Aria skirted around a huge SUV whose back end was sticking way out of its parking space. "Uh . . . yes?" Mike had attended every single Rosewood Day event since they'd returned to Rosewood.

Mike stopped and placed his hands on his hips. A puff of air streamed out of his nostrils. "You mean you haven't heard?" he asked incredulously.

Aria blinked.

Mike sighed. "Skidmarks?" He slapped his palms to his sides. "*Skidz?*"

Aria ran her tongue over her teeth. Come to think of it, she *had* heard that Mike had a new nickname. But she'd figured it was a weird lacrosse ritual.

"Someone planted skidmarked underwear in my locker," Mike moaned, shoving his hands in his jacket pockets and slouching toward the mall's double doors. "They took a photo and texted it to everyone. It's so lame. I don't even *wear* D and G boxer-briefs."

"Do you know who did it?" Aria asked.

"Someone who hates me, I guess."

The hair on Aria's neck rose. It sounded like something A would do. She looked around the parking lot, but it was mostly filled with bedraggled mothers and baby carriages. No one was watching.

"And now everyone's dissing me. They even tried to make me turn in my lacrosse bracelet," Mike went on.

"Did you?" Aria asked, stepping up on the curb.

"No." Mike sounded sheepish. "Noel rallied for me."

Aria felt a little rush of pleasure. "That's nice."

"But I might as well go back to Iceland and join an elf-spotting commune," Mike whined.

Aria snorted and held the door for him. A whoosh of hot air blew her hair back. "It's just a stupid nickname. It will blow over."

Mike sniffed. "Doubt it."

As they walked through the big double doors into Saks, Aria noticed a table off to the left with two small shrines on it: one for Ali, one for Jenna. Memorials like this had popped up in all kinds of places in Rosewood—the local Wawa, a gourmet cheese store on Lancaster Avenue, and the Mighty Quill, a tiny bookshop near Hollis College that Aria and Ali used to visit and covertly read the books about sex. Aria paused, a photo of Jenna catching her eye.

It was the same photo A had sent Emily of Jenna, Ali, and a hidden blond girl they now knew was Courtney. Aria snatched the silver frame and turned it over. How long had this been here? Was this how Billy—or whoever A was—had gotten the photo?

"*Shit,*" Mike whispered sharply, tugging Aria's arm. "Let's go this way." He pivoted to the right and led her toward housewares.

"W-why?" Aria asked.

Mike shot her another nasty look. "*Duh.* I want to avoid Hanna. We broke up."

"Hanna's here?" Aria squeaked, turning her head. And just then, as she peered over her shoulder, she saw Hanna, Spencer, Emily, and Ali standing at the Dior makeup counter. Emily made kissy-faces at the mirror, her cheeks shiny and bright. Spencer leaned over the counter and pointed out a foundation to the salesgirl. Hanna and Ali seemed deep in discussion about shades of eye shadow. They stood in that way that only best friends would. If Aria squinted, Spencer, Hanna, Emily, and Ali could be in seventh grade again. There was just one thing missing: Aria herself.

"Emily, that color looks awesome on you," Ali said.

"We should buy some extra makeup and bring it up to the Poconos after the dance," Spencer said, opening a compact and peering into the little mirror. "We could give each other makeovers."

Aria's heart hurt. It ached to see them having fun

without her, almost like she didn't exist. And had she heard them right--were they seriously going to Ali's Poconos house?

Just think about it, Ali had said to Aria in the woods. *Try to see things from my perspective.* It seemed like the other girls had done just that.

Aria ducked behind a pile of Ralph Lauren cable-knit sweaters and followed Mike away from cosmetics. But as she wound around a table display of crystal vases, Aria couldn't help but remember the first time she and her old friends had raided the Saks makeup counter. It had been a couple days after the Rosewood Charity Drive, when Ali had chosen Aria to be in her new clique. Ali had marched right up to Aria's table and complimented her on the peacock-feather earrings her father had brought her from Spain. It was the first time someone at school had paid Aria a compliment, *especially* someone like Ali. From that day forward, Aria had felt so included, so special. It was amazing to have a tight group of friends—girls who gave her advice, who found her in the halls between classes, who invited her to parties and shopping trips and excursions to the Poconos on the weekends. She'd never forget the time at the Poconos when they'd hidden in one of the secret stairways off a guest bedroom, waiting to scare Jason DiLaurentis when he returned home from hanging out with friends. They'd thought they heard Jason's car in the driveway, and when a plate rattled in the kitchen, Ali burst out of the secret stairway door and cried "Booga

Booga Booga!" But it wasn't Jason—a stray cat had sneaked in through the screen door. Ali had screamed in surprise, and they'd all run back up the stairs and collapsed in a heap on the bed, laughing their heads off. Aria wasn't sure she'd laughed that hard since.

Mike stopped and leaned over a counter, noticing a bunch of stainless steel chronograph watches. Aria peeked across the store at Ali's pale pink, catlike smile. Ali was wearing the same tall, sexy black boots she'd worn the day she'd flirted with Noel in study hall—back when she was still pretending to be Courtney. Suddenly, all Aria could remember was how Ali had gone out with Noel, even though she knew Aria liked him. And how Ali had told Aria that Pigtunia, the stuffed pig Byron had given her, was lame. And how Ali had tormented her about Meredith and Byron's affair.

A door in Aria's mind slammed closed again. All at once, the decision was clear and obvious: Everything was pushing her toward no. For all kinds of reasons, Aria just couldn't put the past behind her like her friends had done. Something about this just wasn't right.

"Come on," Aria said, and this time she was the one to grab Mike's sleeve and pull him out of the store. She didn't trust Ali, and she didn't want her back. And that was that.

21

BLUSH, BONDING, AND BREAKDOWNS

An hour later, Spencer, Ali, Emily, and Hanna were gathered in Spencer's bedroom. Bottles of foundation, trays of blush, and a variety of makeup brushes were splayed out before them. The room smelled better than the inside of Sephora, thanks to their recent raid of the Saks perfume counter. The TV played softly in the background.

"It's not like I threw myself at Wren," Spencer was telling the group, applying a second coat of Bobbi Brown mascara to her top lashes. "We had this instant . . . *connection*. He wasn't right for Melissa at all, but of course she blamed their breakup on me." Ali had asked each of them to fill her in on what had happened while she was away. They had a lot of ground to cover.

Ali splayed her fingers out to admire her freshly applied manicure. "Were you in love with Wren?"

Spencer twirled a tube of mascara between her fingers. Her affair with Wren felt like a million years ago. "Nah."

"What about Andrew?"

The tube of mascara slipped out of Spencer's hand. She felt Hanna's and Emily's eyes on her, too. Part of her still felt certain Ali was going to make fun of Andrew, just like she'd made fun of him in the past.

"I don't know," Spencer answered hesitantly. "Maybe."

Spencer braced herself for Ali's laughter, but to her delight, Ali grabbed Spencer's hands and squealed.

Hanna pressed one of her bed pillows to her chest. "What about you, Ali? Do you miss Ian?"

Ali turned back to the makeup table. "Definitely not."

"How did you guys get together, anyway?" Spencer asked.

"Long story." Ali tested a shade of Chanel lipstick on the side of her hand. "I've moved way on."

"Totally," Hanna piped up, spreading white eye shadow across her eyelids.

"Ancient history." Emily nodded.

Ali laid the lipstick on the dresser. "So are you guys ready for the Poconos tonight?"

"*Absolument,*" Spencer trilled.

"I wish Aria were game," Ali said sadly, pressing her thumb into some spilled powder on the dresser.

"She's been through a lot lately," Emily said, uncapping a bottle of nail polish. "I think she finds it really hard to trust people."

Extreme Makeover suddenly cut out, and the words *Breaking News* flashed across the screen. Spencer looked over, a queasy feeling in her stomach. Every time there was a breaking news segment, it had something to do with her life.

"The new developments in the Rosewood Serial Killer case throw William Ford's guilt into question," a reporter said in an authoritative voice. The Polaroid of the ghostly face in the window of the Hastings barn filled the screen. "Could this be the face of Ms. DiLaurentis's real killer?"

The camera switched to a close-up of Officer Wilden. There were purple circles under his eyes and his skin looked papery. "Our forensic experts have done facial analysis on the new photo found two nights ago. There's a strong chance this is *not* Mr. Ford."

The news reporter popped back on screen and assumed a grave frown. "This data brings up questions about the photos discovered in Mr. Ford's car and on his computer and just how they got there. If anyone has information, please call the police immediately."

The news alert ended, and *Extreme Makeover* resumed. Spencer and the others remained silent. Worry hung over the room like a soupy fog. A chain saw growled in the backyard, followed by the thud of a branch crashing to the ground. A bunch of ducks in the nearby pond quacked.

Ali picked up the remote and turned down the volume. "This is crazy," she said quietly. "Billy killed my sister. I know it."

"Yeah," Hanna said, twisting her hair into a bun. "But that face doesn't look like Billy's."

Ali narrowed her eyes. "Have you ever heard of

Photoshop?"

"You can't Photoshop a Polaroid," Spencer said quietly.

They all exchanged anxious glances. Then Spencer took a deep breath, the image of those glowing blue eyes looming in her mind. A theory had been turning itself around in her head ever since she'd seen that photo. "What if Billy didn't take the pictures?"

"Then who did?" Hanna asked, running her hands up and down her forearms.

Spencer chewed on her pinkie nail. "What if Melissa took them?"

Hanna dropped the blush brush she was holding, sending a cloud of pink powder into the air. Ali cocked her head, a lock of pale blond hair falling in her face. Emily's mouth made a small *O*. No one said a word.

"Sh-she hated you, Ali," Spencer stammered. "Melissa knew you and Ian were dating, and she wanted revenge."

Ali's eyes widened. "What are you saying?"

"That it's possible Melissa took the pictures of us that night—and that she killed Courtney. A couple of weeks ago, before the fire, I saw her hunting around in the woods for something, probably those last few photos. She might have been worried that the police were going to find them during their search for Ian's body. When she couldn't find them, she torched the woods to make sure they were really gone. Except they didn't burn."

Ali stared at Spencer. Her eyes were like saucers.

"It does kind of fit," Emily croaked. "Better than Ian . . . or Jason and Wilden . . . and definitely Billy." Hanna nodded and grabbed Emily's hand.

"Do you think Melissa could've killed Ian, too?" Ali whispered, her face ashen. "And . . . Jenna?"

"I don't know." Spencer thought of the time Ian broke house arrest and met her on her porch. *What if I told you there's something you don't know? It's something big. Something that will turn your life upside down.* Ian had told Spencer that he'd seen two blondes that night. In Spencer's disjointed memories of the evening, she remembered seeing two blondes, too. After Billy was arrested, she'd assumed it was him. But maybe it had been Melissa.

"Maybe Ian and Jenna found out the truth," Spencer said, hugging a pillow to her chest.

Hanna cleared her throat. "I've seen Melissa skulking around lately. I think I saw her at the mall yesterday."

Ali gaped at Hanna. "That person by the fountain?"

Hanna nodded.

Spencer's heart thumped faster and faster. "Do you remember that awful look she gave you at the press conference, Ali? What if Melissa knows you're not Courtney? What if she realizes she got the wrong girl years ago?"

Ali bit her lip. She spun a black Stila eye pencil around and around in her hands. "I don't know. This all sounds crazy. We're talking about your sister. Is she really that unhinged?"

"I have no idea anymore," Spencer admitted.

"Maybe we should just *ask* her. Maybe there's an explanation for all this." Ali stood up.

"Ali, no." Spencer tried to grab Ali's arm. Was Ali insane? What if Melissa *was* the killer and tried to hurt them?

Ali was already at the door. "Strength in numbers," she insisted. "C'mon. We have to end this craziness right now."

Ali marched into the hall, made a left, and knocked on Melissa's bedroom door. No answer. She leaned against it lightly, and it swung open with a long *creak*. The room was in disarray—clothes all over the floor, the bed unmade. Spencer picked Melissa's makeup caddy off the floor. Most of the brushes were dirty, there was loose eye shadow everywhere, and a bottle of moisturizer-with-SPF had leaked onto the bottom of the drawer, making everything smell like the beach.

Ali turned to Spencer. "Do you know where she is?"

"I haven't seen her all day," Spencer said. Which, come to think of it, was a little odd—lately Melissa had been at the house nonstop, tending to their mother's every need.

"Guys, you'd better c'mere," Emily whispered. She was standing at Melissa's desk, staring at something on the computer screen. Spencer and Ali rushed over. The only window open was a jpeg image. It was an old photo of Ian and Ali standing together, Ian's arm around Ali's shoulders. Behind them was the round stone building of the People's Light playhouse, and Spencer could just make out that the marquee said *Romeo and Juliet*. Scrawled over the photo were three simple, chilling words Spencer had definitely seen before.

You're dead, bitch.

Hanna clapped her hand over her mouth. Spencer took a big step away from the computer. Ali sank roughly to Melissa's bed. "I don't understand." Her voice wobbled. "That's *my* photo. What is it doing here?"

"Spencer and I have seen this before." Emily's hands shook. "It was from Mona."

"She put it in my purse," Spencer explained, nausea overcoming her. She staggered to Melissa's desk chair and sat down. "I figured she found this photo in your diary and forged Melissa's handwriting."

Ali shook her head. Her breathing quickened. "Mona didn't do that. That Polaroid showed up in my mailbox years ago—with that writing on it."

Hanna pressed her hand to her chest. "Why didn't you tell us about this?"

"I figured it was a stupid prank!" Ali raised her arms helplessly.

Emily turned back to the computer. She zoomed in on Ali's cheery smile. "But if Mona didn't write this . . . and it's on Melissa's computer . . ." She trailed off.

No one had to complete the sentence. Spencer paced around the room, her mind racing a million miles a minute. "We have to tell Wilden about this. He has to find Melissa and question her."

"Actually . . ." Ali was staring at something on Melissa's bureau. "Maybe we don't have to worry about Melissa right now." She held up a pamphlet. On the front was a logo that said *The Preserve at Addison-Stevens*.

Hanna went pale.

They unfolded the pamphlet on Melissa's bed. It showed a map, outlining the facility's buildings. There was some information about pricing. Clipped to the front was an appointment card for someone named Dr. Louise Foster. Melissa had a meeting with her this morning.

"Dr. Foster," Ali murmured. "She's one of the psychiatrists there."

"Have you tried her cell?" Emily asked, picking up the portable phone on the bed.

Spencer dialed Melissa's phone. "Straight to voice mail."

"Maybe Melissa's decided to check herself in," Ali said, tracing the picture of the main entranceway with her index finger. "Maybe she realized how crazy this was getting and knew she needed help."

Spencer stared at the boxy squares on the map. It was certainly a comforting thought—if Melissa was going to snap, it was best she did so in a padded room. A stay in the psychiatric hospital would probably be the best thing.

A nice *long* stay. Preferably for the next twenty years.

22

TAKE THAT, BITCHES

Hanna parked her Prius at the curb of Ali's house, straightened her dress, and then climbed into Ali's BMW. "Ready?" Ali said, grinning behind the wheel. Wilden had helped her quietly get a license when her parents checked her out of the Preserve.

"Absolutely," Hanna answered.

Her eyes traveled up and down Hanna's mulberry-colored Lela Rose dress, which had a ruffled collar and a cinched waist, and stopped mid-thigh. The dress was even named the Angel, which seemed especially perfect for Valentine's Day. "Ugh," Ali said. "I hate that you look better than me tonight. *Bitch*."

Hanna blushed. "*You're* the one who looks awesome." Dressed in a fitted, lacy red sheath, Ali looked like she could grace the cover of *Vogue*.

Ali shifted the car into drive. They were the only two riding to the dance together—Andrew Campbell was escorting Spencer, and Emily had promised to go with her sister Carolyn. Ali had told Naomi, Riley, and Kate that she was doing an exclusive CNN interview today and would meet them on the dance floor.

The car pulled away from the curb, leaving Ali's dark house behind. For a split second, Hanna swore she saw someone slipping behind one of the pine trees across the street. She thought again about the discussion she, Ali, Emily, and Spencer had had at Spencer's house this afternoon. Could Melissa really have been the stalker behind the barn . . . *and* the murderer?

When they rolled past the stone Rosewood Day sign and up the winding path to the school, she saw girls in swishy gowns strutting down a Valentine-pink carpet that had been laid across the icy road. A couple of kids were doing Hollywood starlet poses as if they were at a movie premiere.

Ali pulled into a parking space, whipped out her cell phone, and hit a speed dial button. Hanna heard a guy's voice on the other end. "You all set?" Ali whispered. "Everyone's getting the papers? Good." She clapped the phone shut and gave Hanna a wicked grin. "Brad and Hayden are manning the doors with the letters." Brad and Hayden were two freshmen she'd conned into helping them.

They got out of the car and started toward the party. As Hanna and Ali passed, Hanna noticed a familiar chiseled profile. Darren Wilden. What the hell was he doing here? Booze police?

"Hi, Hanna," Wilden said, spying her, too. "Long time

no see. Everything okay?"

He was staring at her so curiously that Hanna bristled, wondering if she smelled like champagne. Wilden sometimes got all dadlike because he'd dated Hanna's mom for like a second. "I didn't drive," she snapped.

But Wilden's eyes were now on Ali, who'd moved down the pink carpet. "You and Courtney are friends?" He sounded startled.

Courtney. It was crazy he still thought *that* was her name. "Uh-huh."

Wilden scratched his head. "We've been trying to get Courtney to talk to us about the note she got from Billy the night of the fire. Maybe you could convince her that it's really important."

Hanna pulled her silk scarf tight around her shoulders. "You were the one who rescued her the night of the fire. Why didn't you ask her then?"

Wilden stared across the drive at Rosewood Day's main building, a massive redbrick structure that looked more like an old mansion than a school. "It wasn't exactly the first thing on my mind."

There was a hardened, stern look on his face. A wary feeling swirled in the pit of Hanna's gut as she suddenly remembered how Wilden had played chicken with an oncoming car when he'd driven her home from running a few weeks ago. *Freak.* "Gotta go," Hanna blurted, scampering away.

The inside of the tent was done up in pinks, reds,

and whites, with bouquets of roses everywhere. There were intimate, two-person tables scattered all around the room, complete with votive candles, heart-shaped petit fours, and long-fluted glasses of what Hanna assumed was sparkling cider. Mrs. Betts, one of the art teachers, was giving temporary tattoos in a booth in the corner. Mrs. Reed, the sophomore English teacher, was leaning against the DJ booth, clad in a tight-fitting red gown and heart-shaped sunglasses. There was even an old-fashioned Tunnel of Luv at the far end of the gym. Couples coasted through a makeshift candlelit tunnel in mechanical swans.

Hanna couldn't help but wonder what Mike was doing that night. Something told her he wasn't here.

Ali grabbed her arm. "Look!"

Hanna gazed into the crowd. Guys in red ties and girls in flirty pink and white dresses were staring at the sheets of paper she and Ali had Xeroxed this morning. The whispers began immediately. Jade Smythe and Jenny Kestler nudged each other. Two soccer boys hooted at Riley's use of the word *loins*. Even Mr. Shay, the wizened old biology teacher who chaperoned every Rosewood Day event, chuckled giddily.

"Kate wants to go to V Club!" Kirsten Cullen tittered.

"I always *knew* there was something off about Naomi," exclaimed Gemma Curran.

"*When you touch my arms during blocking, I feel there's a real spark between us,*" Lanie Iler guffawed, reading from Riley's letter to Christophe.

Ali nudged Hanna's side. "Another problem solved by

Ali D!" Her eyes sparkled.

Hanna spied Naomi, Kate, and Riley at the entrance. They were all dressed in identical satin gowns, Kate's bloodred, Naomi's virginal bride white, and Riley's wallflowery blush. They pranced in like princesses.

"*Fag hag!*" someone croaked. Riley looked up, cocking her head like a dog.

"Hey, Naomi, want to see *my* Speedo?" another voice called. Naomi frowned.

A boy passed Kate a pink sheet of paper. She gave it a cursory glance at first, but then her jaw dropped. She nudged Naomi and Riley. Naomi covered her mouth. Riley glared around the room, searching for whoever had done this.

The whisperings and giggles intensified. Hanna squared her shoulders, seizing the opportunity. She marched straight up to Kate. "I thought you should have this." She dropped a silver ring into Kate's limp palm. "It's a purity ring. You'll need it when you join V Club."

The crowd behind Hanna snickered. Hanna signaled to Scott Chin, her old friend on yearbook. He leaped out with his camera and snapped a picture of Kate's horrified face. For once, Hanna was on the right side of the joke. They were laughing *with* her, not at her.

Kate's cheeks bulged, as if she was about to vomit. "You did this, didn't you? You and Courtney."

Hanna shrugged nonchalantly. There was no point in denying it. She turned to Ali, wanting to give credit where credit was due, but Ali was gone.

Kate picked up the crumpled paper from the ground, smoothed it out, and shoved it into her quilted Chanel clutch. "I'm telling Tom about this."

"Tell him," Hanna announced. "I don't care." And then she realized: She *didn't*. So what if Kate told her father? So what if he punished her again? Even if Hanna acted pure and sweet for the rest of her days, her relationship with her dad would never be the same.

Riley flapped her arms up and down like a scrawny chicken. "I get why *you'd* stoop so low, Hanna. But why would Courtney do this? She's our friend."

Hanna leaned against a column decorated with red and white streamers. "Please. You two have had this coming for years."

"Huh?" Naomi huffed. Her boobs were nearly spilling out of her low-cut dress.

The crowd was getting thicker. More and more kids poured into the room and headed to the dance floor. "Courtney wanted to get back at you, obviously," she answered loftily. "For what you did to Ali."

Riley and Naomi exchanged a shocked glance. "*Huh?*" Riley exhaled. Her breath smelled like banana liqueur.

Hanna gazed down her nose at them. "You did something to Ali. That's why she ditched you. This is Courtney's way of getting even."

Heart-shaped confetti suddenly rained magically from the ceiling, sprinkling the top of Naomi's blond hair. She

didn't brush them away. "We didn't do *anything* to Ali."
She shook her head. "One minute, Ali was our best friend.
The next, she acted like she didn't know us at all. I don't
know why she dropped us cold—or why she picked *you* to
replace us. Everyone thought it was a joke, Hanna. You
were *such* a loser."

Hanna bristled. "It wasn't a joke. . . ."

Naomi shrugged. "Whatever. Ali was crazy and a liar,
and her sister obviously is, too. They're *identical* twins, remember? They share everything."

Disco lights spiraled above Hanna's head. She burped,
tasting champagne. Her body felt hot, then cold. What
they were saying couldn't be true.

Naomi and Riley remained rigidly still, waiting for
Hanna's response. Finally, Hanna shrugged. "Whatever,"
she said airily. "We both know you did something terrible,
even if you won't admit it."

Hanna flipped her hair over her shoulder and swiveled
around. "It's your funeral!" Naomi called out as she
walked away. Not that Hanna listened.

23

HURTS SO GOOD

The enormous Valentine's Day dance tent was overflowing with people by the time Emily arrived. Heat lamps were set up along the walls, making the room feel cozy but not stuffy, and a DJ in a red velvet jacket bopped on the stage, mixing a Fergie song into something by Lil Wayne. Mason Byers was swinging Lanie Iler around, Big Band–era style. Nicole Hudson and Kelly Hamilton, Naomi and Riley's on-and-off sophomore toadies, were glaring at each other, annoyed because they'd both worn the same ruffled red gown. A couple of sheets of paper lay on the floor, big shoe marks over them. Emily picked one up. It seemed like a love letter to Sean Ackard. It was signed *Kate Randall*.

Emily straightened the pale pink dress Ali suggested Emily buy from BCBG. She'd gone all out for tonight, blow-drying her hair so that it was sleek and straight, borrowing Carolyn's foundation, blush, and bronzer to make her skin look glowing and sparkly. She'd forced her flat, flipper-like swimmer's feet into a pair of red Mary Janes she'd worn only once to a sports banquet. Emily wanted Ali to be dazzled by the sight of her.

A knot of kids gyrated on the dance floor. Andrew Campbell spun Spencer around, their hands entwined. Hanna had her arms in the air and was doing a slinky, sexy dance Emily could never pull off. The girl next to her was dressed in a gorgeous, lacy red gown, her hair piled seductively on her head. *Ali.* Then she noticed James Freed standing behind Ali, snaking his hands along her hips, up her waist, and dangerously close to her boobs.

It took Emily a couple of seconds to realize what was happening. Her heart lurched. But by the time she'd marched over to the circle, James had peeled off and started dancing on his own, doing a faux Justin Timberlake move that involved spinning on one heel.

"Hey," Emily said in Ali's ear.

Ali opened her eyes. "Hey, Em!" She kept dancing.

Emily paused, waiting. Surely Ali would do a double take. Certainly she'd blurt out, *Oh my God, you look incredible!* But now Ali was whispering something to Hanna. Hanna threw her auburn head back and cackled.

"For all you Valentines out there," crooned the DJ as a slow, bluesy John Mayer song came on. Spencer hugged Andrew's waist. Hanna danced with Mason Byers. Emily stared meaningfully at Ali's back, but Ali still didn't turn around. She fell into James's arms as if they'd been a couple for years. They began rocking back and forth to the music.

A couple bumped into Emily from behind. She staggered to the side of the dance floor. Ali had said she . . . the other day at her house . . . *I meant what I said about how I feel about you.* A cold sweat crept down Emily's neck. Did Ali mean it . . . or didn't she?

Couples were disappearing into a smaller tent that said TUNNEL OF LUV toward the back. Rosewood Day had trotted out the creaky ride since Emily was in fifth grade, renting it from a local carnival supply company. The ride had about ten plastic swans, big enough for two people. The swans were so old that their yellow beaks were now a jaundiced tan, and much of the paint on their white bodies had flaked off entirely.

The slow song droned on for another agonizing three minutes. When it ended, Ali and James broke apart, laughing softly. Emily leaped into their path and caught Ali's arm. "I need to talk to you."

Ali smiled. The disco light reflected off her shimmery eye shadow. "Sure. What's up?"

"*Alone.*"

Emily dragged her through the exit that led into the school and turned left to the girls' room. All the stall doors were flung open, and the room smelled like a phantom mix of various perfumes and makeup. Ali leaned over the sink, inspecting her mascara.

"Why are you being like this?" Emily blurted before

she'd fully planned what she was going to say.

Ali cocked her head, meeting Emily's eyes in the mirror. "Like what?"

"You're ignoring me."

"No, I'm not!"

Emily slapped her sides. "Ali, yes, you *are*."

The corners of Ali's mouth turned down. She put a finger to her lips. "Call me Courtney, remember?"

"Fine. *Courtney*."

Emily whirled around and faced the automatic hand dryer, staring at her warped reflection in the metal. It was like they'd taken ten steps backward. Emily's limbs started to quake. Her stomach churned. Her skin felt like it was under a hot broiler.

She turned around to face Ali again. "You know, friends don't jerk friends around. Friends don't give each other mixed messages. And . . . and I don't think I can handle being friends if things are going to be the same as they were before."

Ali looked shocked. "I don't *want* things to be the same. I want them to be better."

"They aren't better!" Wet, sweaty patches bloomed under the arms of Emily's brand-new pink dress. "They're worse!"

Ali sunk into one hip. A defeated look crossed her face. "Nothing is good enough for you, Em," she said wearily, her shoulders sinking.

"Ali," Emily whispered. "I'm sorry." She reached out

and touched Ali's arm, but Ali bristled and shook her off.

But then Ali turned back, her arms hanging limply at her sides. Ever so slowly, Ali took a step toward Emily. Her lips quivered. The corners of her eyes were wet. They stared at each other for a static-filled moment, Emily barely breathing. And then, Ali yanked Emily into an empty stall and pressed their bodies close. They kissed and kissed, the world melting away, the music from the dance subsiding until it was a dull echo. After a moment, they pulled back, breathless. Emily stared at Ali's shiny eyes.

"What was *that* for?" she asked.

Ali reached out and touched the tip of Emily's nose. "I'm sorry, too," she whispered.

24

MISSING PERSONS

About an hour later, as the dance was drawing to a close, Andrew and Spencer climbed into a bobbing ivory swan and set off into the Tunnel of Luv. The water beneath them smelled like lavender. Fairy lights were strewn around the entrance of the tunnel. As they floated into darkness, soft harp music nearly drowned out the techno song on the dance floor.

"I can't believe this ride still works." Spencer rested her head on Andrew's shoulder.

Andrew laced his fingers through hers. "I wouldn't complain if it broke down and stranded us here for a couple hours."

"Oh yeah?" Spencer teased, punching him playfully on the arm.

"Yeah." Andrew's lips found hers, and she kissed him back. A warm feeling of well-being slowly pulsed through Spencer's veins. Finally, everything in her life was right—she had a great boyfriend, a fantastic sister, *and* her best friends back. It almost didn't feel real.

The ride ended way too quickly, and Andrew helped Spencer out of the swan. She checked her watch. Ali wanted them to meet at her car in five minutes. She leaned in to kiss Andrew good-bye. "See you tomorrow," she whispered. She was dying to tell him the truth about Ali, but she'd promised to keep her mouth shut.

"Have fun," Andrew said, kissing her softly.

Spencer turned and started for the door, then teetered to where Ali's BMW was parked. She was the first one there, so she leaned against the trunk and waited. It was freezing out and her eyes started to tear. Emily skipped up next. Her hair was mussed, her makeup was smudged, but she looked overjoyed. "Hey," she chirped. "Where's Ali?"

"Not here yet," Spencer answered. She crossed her arms over her chest, hoping Ali would show up soon. Her feet were quickly turning to ice.

Hanna arrived next. A few minutes passed. Spencer pulled out her cell phone and checked the time: 9:40. Ali had instructed that they meet her at 9:30, sharp.

"I'll text her," Emily said, typing into her phone.

A moment later, Spencer's phone bleated loudly, making everyone jump. She lunged for it, but it was her home phone number.

"Have you seen Melissa?" Mrs. Hastings asked when she picked up the line. "I haven't seen her all day. I've tried her cell phone a few times, too, but it's gone straight to voice mail. That never happens."

Spencer gazed toward the tent. Kids were streaming into the parking lot, but Ali wasn't among them.

"You haven't gotten any calls from a hospital?" Spencer said into the phone. If someone had checked herself into the Preserve, the staff would have to notify family so they wouldn't worry, right?

"A hospital?" Mrs. Hastings's voice peaked sharply. "Why? Is she hurt?"

Spencer squeezed her eyes shut. "I don't know."

Mrs. Hastings told Spencer to call her immediately if she heard from Melissa, then abruptly hung up. Spencer could feel her old friends' eyes on her. "Who was that?" Emily asked quietly.

Spencer didn't answer. The *You're dead, bitch* photo floated into her mind once more. The last time she'd seen Melissa was when her sister had driven her to school and warned her to be careful with Courtney. After that, Melissa had been oddly absent. Was she at the Preserve . . . or was she somewhere else? What if she was *here*—watching Ali *right now*?

"Is everything okay?" Hanna asked.

There was a golf ball–size lump in Spencer's throat. She gazed toward the tent again, desperately hoping to see Ali's blond head among the crowds of kids.

"Everything's fine," she murmured, her heart beating faster and faster. There was no use getting everyone freaked out quite yet. *Come on, Ali,* she thought frantically. *Where are you?*

25

TRUE COLORS SHINING THROUGH

After waiting about fifteen minutes in a long girls'
bathroom line, Aria emerged on the dance floor and
gazed around the room for Noel. He'd been a gentleman
all night, dancing every dance with her, getting her glasses
of pink punch whenever she was thirsty, already talking
about how they were going to go all out for prom—maybe
they could even arrive by his dad's helicopter. Everything
just felt . . . *right*.

She pushed her way toward the bar, figuring Noel might
be there. Kids swirled around her, their dresses swishing.
With so much red, pink, and white, Aria felt like she was
inside a giant circulatory system. A few kids stared as she
passed, smirks on their faces. A knot of sophomore girls
nudged one another and whispered. Mason Byers caught
sight of Aria, widened his eyes, and turned away. Aria's
heart began to thump. What the hell was going on?

And suddenly, as if on cue, the crowd parted. In the
corner of the tent, right next to the chocolate dipping

station, a couple stood kissing. One of them had slicked-back dark hair and wore a gorgeous black suit. The other was sylph-thin, with honey blond hair done up in a French twist. Her fitted red cocktail dress skimmed her hips. The surface of her skin sparkled, as if it had been brushed with diamond dust.

Aria watched helplessly as the music swirled romantically. Someone let out a loud whoop.

Time snapped into warp speed, and just as a fiery flame ignited in Aria's stomach, Ali broke away from Noel, her face twisted with outrage. She slapped him hard, her hand making a loud cracking sound against his cheek. "What are you doing?" she screamed as Aria rushed over.

"Wha . . . ?" Noel stammered. A huge red welt appeared where Ali had slapped him. "I don't . . ."

"Aria is my friend!" Ali screamed. "Who the hell do you think I am?"

Then she turned, locked eyes with Aria, and froze. Her lips parted. Noel turned and saw Aria, too. His face went sheet-white. He started to shake his head, as if to say he didn't know how he'd found himself here, doing what he was doing. Aria glared from Noel to Ali, her fingers twitching with rage.

The cloying scent of dark chocolate from the fondue station wafted into Aria's nostrils. The oscillating spotlight on the dance floor turned Ali and Noel from blue to red to yellow. Aria was so angry that her teeth began to chatter.

Noel's Adam's apple bobbed. Ali stood a safe

distance away, shaking her head both self-righteously and sympathetically. "Aria, it's not . . ." Noel started.

"You said she didn't matter," Aria interrupted. Her chin wobbled, but she steeled herself not to cry. "You said you didn't like her. You wanted me to give her a *chance.*"

"Aria, wait!" Noel's voice cracked. But she didn't let him finish, whirling away and weaving around the gaping partygoers. Lucas Beattie let out a gasp. Zelda Millings, who went to the nearby Quaker school but *always* managed to snag dates to Rosewood Day events, smirked. *Let them,* Aria thought. She didn't care.

Aria was almost to the door when she felt a hand on her arm. It was Ali. "I'm so sorry." She panted, out of breath. "He just . . . *smothered* me. There was nothing I could do about it."

Aria kept walking on, too furious to speak. Her instincts about Noel had been right all along. He was a typical, lacrosse-playing, fratty, cheating Rosewood boy. He'd claimed to be different and she'd *bought* it. She was *so* stupid.

Ali was still keeping pace with Aria, her arms crossed and her head bowed. *I've changed,* Ali had said at the wishing well. Maybe she had.

They emerged into the frigid air. A bunch of kids loitered near their cars, smoking cigarettes. Fireworks erupted above the stately school, marking the end of the dance. Across the parking lot, Aria spied Spencer, Emily, and Hanna leaning against a BMW. Their faces brightened when they saw Ali, and Ali waved back.

Aria knew what her old friends were waiting for and where they would be going next. Suddenly, she realized how badly she wanted to join them. How badly she wanted to go back to the way things were—before all the secrets and lies. Back to when they first became friends and everything was filled with possibility.

"Um, about your Poconos trip," she said tentatively, not daring to look Ali in the eye. "Do you think there's room for one more?"

The corners of Ali's mouth spread into a wide grin. She jumped up and down a little, and then threw her arms around Aria's shoulders. "I thought you'd never ask."

Ali pulled Aria across the parking lot, avoiding a shiny patch of ice. "We're going to have such a great time, I promise. You'll forget all about Noel. And tomorrow, we'll find you someone even hotter."

They skipped to the bottom of the hill, arm in arm. "Look who I found!" Ali cried, hitting the unlock button on her key chain. "She's coming with us!"

Everyone whooped. Suddenly, Aria heard a strange, muffled sound. She paused, curling her hand over the car door. It sounded like a thump, followed by a squeal.

"Did you hear that?" she whispered, looking around the parking lot. Couples staggered to their cars. Limos chugged. Mothers waited for their kids in their SUVs. Aria thought about the Polaroids she'd found in the woods. That phantom face, looming at the barn window. She looked around for Wilden . . . or any cop, for that matter, but they were all gone.

Ali paused. "Hear what?"

Aria waited, listening again. Between the thumping bass and the booming fireworks, it was difficult to hear anything. "I guess it's nothing," she decided. "Probably just some kids hooking up on the Commons."

"Sluts," Ali giggled. She opened her door and gracefully got into the driver's seat. Spencer sat beside her, and Hanna, Emily, and Aria clambered into the back. As soon as the car flickered to life, Ali cranked the music up so loud that it drowned out the fireworks. "Let's go, bitches!" she cried. And off they went.

26

A REINVENTION OF THE PAST

The DiLaurentises' Poconos house was exactly as Hanna remembered it: large and rambling, with red-painted teak siding and white shutters and windows. The porch light was off, but the moon was so big and bright that Hanna could see five white rockers on the porch. She, Ali, and the others used to sit on those rockers, *Us Weekly* magazines in their laps, watching the sun set over the lake.

The car crunched into the driveway and rolled to a stop. Everyone leaped up and grabbed their purses. The night air was cold. A mist hung over the valley, as fine and vaporous as breath.

There was a rustle in the bushes. Hanna halted. A long tail flickered. Two eyes glowed yellow. A black cat scampered stealthily across the driveway and into the woods. She breathed out.

Ali unlocked the door to the house and ushered them in. The place smelled like aged wallpaper glue, dusty wood floors, and closed-up rooms. There was also a faint odor that reminded Hanna of old hamburger.

"Drinks?" Ali cried, dropping the keys on the farmhouse table.

"Definitely," Spencer said. She unloaded a grocery bag of Cheez-Its, blue corn tortilla chips, M&M's, Diet Coke, Red Bull, and a bottle of vodka. Hanna went to the cupboard where the DiLaurentises kept their glasses and pulled out five crystal tumblers.

After making vodka and Red Bulls, everyone strolled into the den. Built-in bookshelves lined the walls. The closet was slightly open, revealing stacks and stacks of old board games. The television that got only four channels still sat on the old hutch. Hanna stared out at the big backyard, immediately locating the spot where they'd built the five-girl tent and slept under the stars. Ali had presented them with their Jenna bracelets in that tent, making them promise that they'd remain best friends until the day they died.

Hanna wandered over to the mantel, noticing a familiar silver-framed photo. It was the picture of the five of them standing next to a big canoe, all of them soaking wet. The same photo used to hang in the DiLaurentises' old foyer. It had been taken the first time Ali invited them to the Poconos, not long after they became friends. Hanna and the others had made up a secret ritual of touching the bottom corner of the photo at the same time, though they'd been too embarrassed to tell Ali about it.

Everyone else gathered around the photo, too. The

ice in their glasses rattled. "Remember that day?" Emily murmured. Her breath already smelled like vodka. "That crazy waterfall?"

Hanna snorted. "Yeah. You freaked." It was their maiden voyage on a new canoe Mr. DiLaurentis had bought from the local sporting goods store. They'd all paddled furiously to start off, but then everyone got tired and bored and let the current carry them. When the river began to get rough, Spencer wanted to try and ride the rapids. Then Emily saw the little waterfall ahead and demanded they abandon ship.

Spencer nudged Emily's ribs. "You were like, 'People die if they go over waterfalls in a canoe! We should tip it and swim to shore!'"

"And then you tipped us all without telling us first," Aria said, shaking with giggles. "That water was *so* cold!"

"I was shivering for days," Emily agreed.

"We look so young," Hanna murmured, focusing especially on her own pudgy face. "Just think, a couple weeks before that, we were sneaking into your yard trying to steal your flag, Ali."

"Yeah," Ali said distractedly. Hanna watched her, waiting for Ali to chime in with a memory, but Ali simply began to pull out the bobby pins from her French twist, setting each one on the glass end table. Maybe it was wrong to bring up the Time Capsule day. Courtney had apparently been home that weekend, switching from the Radley to the Preserve. It probably stirred up all kinds of bad memories.

Hanna looked at the photo again. Things had been so different then. When they'd tipped the canoe, Hanna's drenched, oversize T-shirt had clung to every roll of skin and ounce of fat. Not long after, Ali began to make remarks about how Hanna ate so much more than the rest of them, and that Hanna didn't play a sport, and that Hanna always went for seconds at lunch. Once, at the King James Mall, she'd even quipped that they should go into Faith 21—Forever 21's plus-size store—just to "look around."

Suddenly, Naomi's words flashed through Hanna's mind. *Everyone said Ali picked you as a joke. You were such a loser.*

Hanna slumped against the sideboard, nearly knocking over a decorative plate adorned with a print of Independence Mall. Her mouth felt sticky with vodka, and her limbs hung loose and free.

Ali turned and lobbed something white and fluffy at each of the girls. "Hot tub time!" She clapped her hands. "Make yourselves fresh cocktails and get changed while I go outside and turn it on."

Grabbing her drink, Ali skipped through the living room and out to the back porch, her blond ponytail bobbing. Hanna stared at the objects Ali had thrown at her—a fluffy white Frette towel and a polka-dotted Marc Jacobs string bikini. She held the bikini top and bottom up to the light, admiring the shiny fabric and silvery ties.

Hanna straightened up, suddenly refortified. *Nice try, bitches.* The tag inside the butt read size zero. Hanna smiled to herself, flattered and stunned. It was the best compliment anyone could have given her.

27

BEST FRIENDS FOREVER

The alcohol had definitely gone to Emily's head. She stood in the tiny Pennsylvania Dutch–themed downstairs bathroom clad in only her string bikini, tilting from one side to the other, sizing up her toned biceps, her thin waist, and her shapely shoulders. "You're hot," she whispered to her reflection. "Ali wants you." She started to giggle.

Not only was she drunk on vodka, she was also drunk on *Ali*. It was thrilling to be back in the Poconos. And kissing Ali at the dance? Emily wasn't sure when she'd felt happier in her entire life.

Emily marched out of the bathroom, a fluffy white towel wrapped around her waist. She plucked a half-drunk cocktail off the buffet table and skipped out to the three-season porch. It was exactly as she remembered it—the overpowering smell of potting soil and wetness, the stone garden gnomes in the corner, and the quirky, chipped tile-top tables Mrs. DiLaurentis had found at an estate sale. Emily expected to see Ali there—she'd wanted to give Ali a secret kiss before the others came out—but the room was empty.

"Chilly!" Emily cried as her bare toes hit the frigid floor. A heat lamp had been set up near the door, and the big green plastic cover had been pulled off the hot tub. The motor groaned loudly. Bluish bubbles rose to the surface of the tub. When Emily touched the water, she squealed again. It was ice-cold. The tub probably hadn't been used in years.

Hanna, Spencer, and Aria emerged onto the porch. As they waited for Ali to change, Hanna dragged in the iPod speakers from the living room and put on Britney Spears, who they'd loved dancing to in seventh grade. They all sang along to the music, just like old times. Emily stretched her towel out, sliding it seductively down the length of her bikini-clad body. Hanna strutted up and down the porch like she was on the catwalk, pausing at the end of the room to pose. Spencer did high Rockette-style kicks. Aria tried to imitate her and almost took out a dead fern. The girls doubled over laughing, wrapping their arms around one another. They leaned against the side of the hot tub, gasping for breath.

"I can't believe we didn't talk to each other for so many years," Spencer blurted. "What was *wrong* with us?"

Aria waved her hand with an uninhibited flourish. "We were stupid. We should've stayed friends."

Emily's face flushed. "Seriously," she whispered. She'd had no idea the others felt the same way she did.

Hanna brushed a couple of dead leaves off one of the

outdoor chairs and plopped down. "I missed you guys."

"No, you didn't." Spencer pointed at her drunkenly. "You had Mona."

They all fell silent, ruminating on what Mona had done to all of them. Emily felt a lump in her throat as she watched Hanna wince and turn away. It was bad enough that Mona had tormented Emily, but Mona had been Hanna's best friend.

Emily stepped forward and wrapped her arms around Hanna. "I'm so sorry," she whispered. Spencer moved in next, and then Aria. "She was insane," Spencer murmured.

"I should have never lost touch with you guys," Hanna mumbled into Spencer's shoulder.

"It's okay," Emily cried, petting Hanna's long, silky hair. "You have us now."

They remained that way until the song petered out into silence. The hot tub groaned. A loud *thump* sounded from inside the house. Spencer looked up, her brow furrowing. "Ali sure is taking a long time to change."

Everyone wrapped their towels around their shoulders and went inside. They moved through the living room and into the kitchen. "Ali?" Hanna called. No answer. Emily poked her head into the bathroom from which she'd just emerged. Water dripped from the faucet. The heat from the vent made the tail of the toilet paper roll float in the air.

"Ali?" Aria called into the formal sitting room. Sheets

had been draped over the chairs, making them look like lumpish ghosts. Everyone stood stock-still, listening.

Spencer paused in the kitchen. "Maybe I shouldn't be bringing this up now, but my mom called earlier. My sister is still missing. . . ."

"*What?*" Emily stopped next to the stove.

"What if she followed us?" Spencer's voice wobbled. "What if she's here?"

"She can't be." Hanna took a fortifying swig of her cocktail. "Spencer, there's no way."

Spencer pulled her sweater over her head and padded toward the door that led to the side yard. Emily grabbed her sweatshirt and jeans, pulled them on, and followed. The old, rusty side door creaked as it opened. The sky was bright with stars. The only other light was a single golden beam from the garage. The black BMW was parked in the driveway. Emily's eyes flickered back and forth, searching desperately for a shifting shadow. She pulled out her phone, wondering if they should call someone. Her screen said *No Service Available.* Everyone else looked at their phones, too, and shook their heads. They were all out of range.

Emily shivered. *This can't be happening. Not again.* What if they'd been on the sun porch, having a great time, and something awful had happened to Ali? It was like a repeat of seventh grade: For minutes they'd sat in the barn, dumbly hypnotized, while a girl had been murdered.

"Ali!" Emily cried out. The name echoed into the

night. "Ali!" she called again.

"What?" came a voice.

Everyone whipped around. Ali was standing in the kitchen doorway, still dressed in her jeans and cashmere hoodie. She was looking at them like they were crazy.

"Where have you guys *been*?" Ali laughed. "I just went to check the temperature in the hot tub, and I couldn't find you anywhere!" She pretended to wipe sweat from her brow. "I was so scared!"

Emily walked back into the house, breathing a long sigh of relief. But as Ali held the door for her, giving her a huge, bright smile, Emily heard a branch snap from behind. She froze and glanced over her shoulder, certain she would see a pair of eyes gazing at her from the dense woods.

But everything was still and quiet. There was no one.

28

WHAT DREAMS MAY COME

Spencer and the others followed Ali back into the house. "The hot tub is way too cold," Ali decided. "But there are lots of other things to do."

Spencer plopped her unused bath towel on the kitchen table, walked into the living room, and sat down on the leather couch. Her skin felt numb, both from the cold and the scare that something might have happened to Ali. An uneasy feeling nagged at her, too, one she couldn't quite describe. How had Ali not heard them when they were calling for her? How had they not seen her go into the porch and test the water of the hot tub? What was that *thump* they'd heard inside the house? And where *was* Melissa, anyway?

The other girls gathered around the room. Ali sat in the wicker wing chair they used to call "The Duchess Chair": whichever girl they deemed the "Duchess" got to sit in the chair and make the others do whatever she wanted for the entire day. Hanna sat on the old yellow beanbag near the TV. Emily perched cross-legged on the leather ottoman by the couch, absently poking her finger into a tiny hole in the upholstery. Aria sat on the couch next to Spencer and pulled a cherry-blossom-printed satin pillow into her chest.

Ali curled her hands around the Duchess Chair's twisted, twiggy arms and took a big breath. "So. Now that the hot tub idea is a bust, I have a proposition for you."

"What?" Spencer asked.

Ali shifted her weight, making the wicker creak. "Since our last sleepover went so badly, I think we should wipe it out of our minds for good. I'd like to re-create it. Minus a couple of details, of course."

"Like you disappearing?" Emily said.

"Naturally." Ali twirled a piece of hair around her finger. "And, well, for it to be accurate, I'll have to hypnotize you."

Spencer's skin went cold. Emily lowered her glass to the table. Hanna froze, a handful of Cheez-Its halfway to her mouth. "Uh . . ." Aria started.

Ali cocked an eyebrow. "When I was in the hospital, they made me go to all these therapists. One of them told me that the best way to get over a terrible memory is to reenact it. I really think it will help me. . . ." She sighed. "Maybe it will help all of us."

Spencer rubbed her feet together, trying to warm them up. A sudden wind whistled outside. She stared again at the photo of them next to the canoe. Reenacting the hypnosis sounded awful, but maybe Ali was right. After everything they'd been through, maybe they needed to do something to get past it, once and for all. "I'm game," she decided.

"Yeah, I guess I'm in, too," Emily decided.

"Sure," Hanna said.

Ali looked hopefully at Aria, and Aria nodded reluctantly. "Thank you." Ali jumped to her feet. "Let's do it in the upstairs bedroom, though. It's more intimate. More like the barn was."

They followed her up the pink-carpeted stairs to the second level. A huge, pale moon shone through the circular window on the landing. The yard was empty, the pine trees forming a thick barrier between the house and the road. There was a man-made pond off to the left, though it had been drained for the winter. Now it was merely a dry, deep ditch.

Ali led them to the back bedroom. The door was already ajar, as if someone had been in here recently. Spencer remembered the cross-stitch sampler on the wall, the Queen Anne's lace curtains, and the twin brass beds. Her nose twitched. She'd expected the room to be redolent with lilac-scented air freshener and maybe mildew, but there was a rotting, curdling odor instead. "What's that smell?" she cried.

Ali wrinkled her nose, too. "Maybe there's something dead inside the walls. Remember when that happened the summer between sixth and seventh grades? I think it was a raccoon."

Spencer racked her brain, but she didn't remember smelling anything remotely like this before.

Then Aria froze. "Did you hear that?"

Everyone tensed, listening. "No . . ." Spencer whispered.

Aria's eyes were wide. "I think I heard someone cough. Is there someone outside?"

Ali peeled back a wooden slat in the blinds. The driveway was deserted. There were tracks in the gravel from where the BMW had pulled in. "Nothing," Ali whispered.

They all let out a long sigh. "We're psyching ourselves out," Spencer said. "We've got to calm down."

They plopped on the round rug on the floor. Ali pulled out six vanilla candles from a plastic bag and positioned them on the nightstands and the bureau. The match made a spitting sound as it ignited. The room was already dark, but Ali twisted the blinds closed and pulled the curtains tight. The candles cast eerie shadows on the wall.

"Okay," Ali said. "Um, everyone, just relax."

Emily giggled anxiously. Hanna let out a breath. Spencer tried to make her arms go limp, but her blood still zoomed in her ears. She'd relived the moment Ali had hypnotized her so many times in her mind. Every time she thought about it, her body contorted with panic. *You'll be fine,* she told herself.

"Your heartbeat's slowing down," Ali chanted. "Think calm thoughts. I'm going to count down from one hundred, and as soon as I touch all of you, you'll be in my power."

No one spoke. The candles snapped and danced. Spencer shut her eyes as Ali began to count. "One hundred . . . ninety-nine . . . ninety-eight . . . "

Spencer's left leg twitched, then her right. She tried to think calm thoughts, but it was impossible not to return to the night they'd done this last. She'd sat on the round rug in her family's barn, pissed off that Ali had yet again talked them into something they didn't want to do. What if Ali's hypnosis made her blurt out she'd kissed Ian . . . and Melissa heard? Melissa and Ian had just been in the barn—they still could be close by.

And maybe, just maybe, Melissa *had* been close by. Like at the window . . . with a camera.

"Eighty-five, eighty-four . . ." Ali lilted.

Her voice faded farther and farther away until it sounded like she was whispering from the end of a very long tunnel. Then smudged light appeared before Spencer's eyes. Sound warped and twisted. The smell of sanded floorboards and microwave popcorn tickled her nose. She took a few long, deep breaths, trying to imagine air flowing in and out of her lungs.

When Spencer's vision came into focus, she realized she was in her family's old barn. She was sitting on the old, soft rug her parents had bought in New York. The scent of pine and early summer flowers wafted in from outside. She looked at her friends. Hanna's stomach bulged. Emily was bone thin and freckly. Aria had streaks of pink in her hair. Ali tiptoed among them, touching their foreheads with the fleshy part of her thumb. When she got to Spencer, Spencer jumped up.

It's too dark in here, she heard herself saying. The words spilled out of her mouth, beyond her control.

No, Ali insisted. *It's got to be dark. That's how it works.*

It doesn't always have to be the way you want it, you know, Ali? Spencer told her.

Close them, Ali answered, baring her teeth.

Spencer struggled to let light into the room. Ali let out a frustrated groan. But when Spencer glanced back at Ali, she realized that Ali wasn't just angry. She'd frozen in place, her face drawn and ghost-pale, her eyes round. It was like she'd seen something awful.

Spencer turned back to the window, a shadow catching her eye. It was a tiny shard of a memory, barely anything. Spencer clung to the image now, desperate to remember whether it had really happened. And then . . . she saw. It was Ali's reflection . . . except she wore a hood and carried a bulky camera. Her eyes were demonic and unblinking, out for murder. It was someone Spencer knew very well. She tried to say her name, but her lips wouldn't work. She felt like she was choking.

The memory was rolling forward without her. *Leave,* she heard herself demand to Ali.

Fine, Ali answered.

"No!" Spencer told her old self. "Call Ali back! Keep

her in the room! It's . . . it's her *sister* out there! And she wants to hurt Ali!"

But the memory careened on, out of Spencer's grasp. Ali was at the door now. She turned around, giving Spencer a long look. Spencer let out a hoarse gasp. Suddenly, Ali didn't quite look like the girl who was with them today.

Then Spencer's gaze fell to the silver ring on the girl's finger. Ali had said she hadn't been wearing a ring that night, but there it was. Only, except instead of an *A* in the center, there was a *C*.

Why did Ali have on the wrong ring?

There was a tap on the window, and Spencer turned. The girl outside smiled sinisterly, running a hand along her eerily identical heart-shaped face. She held up the fourth finger on her right hand. She was wearing a ring, too—hers with the initial *A*. Spencer's head felt like it was going to explode. Was Ali out there . . . and Courtney in here? How had *that* happened?

My memory's playing tricks on me, she told herself. *This didn't happen. It's just a dream.*

The Ali at the door turned, her hand on the knob. Suddenly, her skin began to fade from pink to pale to white to ashen. "Ali?" Spencer called out cautiously. "Are you okay?"

Ali's skin had begun to flake off in thick curls. "Does it look like I'm okay?" she snapped. She shook her head at Spencer. "I've been trying to tell you . . ."

"Trying to tell me?" Spencer echoed. "What do you mean?"

"All those dreams you've had about me? Don't you remember?"

Spencer blinked. "I . . ."

Ali rolled her eyes. Her skin was peeling off faster now, revealing ropy muscles and bleached bones. Her teeth plunked to the floor like acorns. Her hair turned from golden blond to pale gray. Then it started to fall out in chunks. "You really *are* stupider than I thought, Spence," she hissed. "You deserve this."

"Deserve what?" Spencer screamed.

Ali didn't answer. When she turned the knob, her hand flaked off at the elbow, as brittle as a dried flower. It landed on the wood floor and promptly dissolved into dust. Then the door slammed hard, the force resonating through Spencer's body. It sounded close. *Real.* Memory and reality collided.

Spencer's eyes sprang open. The bedroom was oppressively hot; sweat poured down her face. Her old friends sat cross-legged on the carpet, their faces docile and relaxed, their eyes sealed shut. They looked . . . dead.

"Guys?" Spencer called. No answer. She wanted to reach out and touch Hanna, but she was afraid.

The dream crackled in her brain. *I've been trying to tell you,* the girl in the vision said. The one who looked like the Ali she remembered . . . but the one who was wearing Courtney's ring. *All those dreams you've had about me. Don't you remember?*

Spencer did remember plenty of dreams about Ali. Sometimes, she even dreamed about two *different* Alis.

"No," Spencer whispered perilously. She didn't understand this. She blinked in the darkness, looking for her fourth friend.

"Ali?" she squeaked.

But Ali didn't answer. Because Ali was gone.

29

THE LETTER UNDER THE DOOR

Aria heard a slam and jerked awake. Half the candles had blown out. A putrid smell filled the air. Her three old best friends were sitting on the carpet, staring at her.

"What's going on?" she asked. "Where's Ali?"

"We don't know." Emily looked terrified. "She . . . disappeared."

"Maybe this is part of the reenactment?" Hanna suggested groggily.

"I don't think so, guys." Spencer's voice trembled. "I think something's really wrong."

"Of course something's wrong!" Emily cried. "Ali's gone!"

"No," Spencer said. "I think . . . I think something's wrong with *Ali*."

Aria gaped at her. "Ali?" Emily sputtered.

"What do you mean?" Hanna demanded.

"I think the girl at the window of the barn was Ali's sister," Spencer whispered, her voice thick with sobs. "I think that's who killed her."

Hanna wrinkled her brow. "I thought you said it was Melissa."

"And no one killed Ali," Emily added, narrowing her eyes. "She's *here*."

But Aria stared at Spencer, a tiny kernel of an idea forming in her head. She thought of those Polaroids again. It could have been a DiLaurentis face reflected in the window.

"Oh my God," Aria whispered, remembering what that creepy medium had said to her a few weeks ago, as she stood over the hole where Ali's body had been found: *Ali killed Ali.*

A *bang* thundered from downstairs. Everyone jumped and scuttled back into the corner, hugging one another tight. "What was *that*?" Hanna whispered.

There were a few more creaks and slams, then silence. Aria dared to look around the rest of the room. Someone must have opened the curtains, because moonlight spilled through the window onto the floor. That was when she noticed something she hadn't seen before. Just inches from the door was a white envelope. It looked as though someone had recently slipped it through the crack.

"Um, guys?" she squeaked, pointing a shaky finger at it.

Everyone stared, too petrified to move. Finally, Spencer snatched it off the ground. Her fingers shook. She held the front of the envelope out for the rest of them to see.

To: Four Bitches. From: A.

Emily sank to her knees. "Oh my God. It's Billy. He's here."

"It's *not* Billy," Spencer snapped.

"Then it's Melissa," Emily guessed frantically.

Spencer tore open the note. Lines and lines of type covered the page. As she read, her mouth twisted. "Oh my God."

Hanna squinted. "This can't be real."

A cold, hard knot of certainty congealed in the pit of Aria's stomach. There was something wrong. Taking a deep breath, she leaned in and read, too.

Once upon a time, there were two beautiful girls named Ali and Courtney—but one of them was crazy. And as you know, with a few magical twists of fate, Ali became Courtney for a while. But what you don't know is that Courtney became Ali, too.

You heard me right, Pretty Little Losers . . . and it's all because of you. Remember when you stalked me in my backyard for the Time Capsule flag? And remember that girl who trotted out to the lawn and talked to you? That wasn't me. As you so astutely figured out, Courtney was home switching from the Radley to the Preserve that weekend. And oh, how poor widdle Courtney didn't want to go. She had her neat, crazy little life at the Radley . . . and she didn't want to start over in a new hospital.

If she had to start over somewhere, it was going to be in Rosewood. And start over she did. She was supposed to go to the Preserve the very morning she saw you skulking around my yard—and man, did she jump on the chance fast. One minute, she and I were arguing—I was so happy she was on her way out—and the next she was in the yard, pretending to be me, talking to you guys like you were BFFs. Talking about my flag as if she hadn't been the one who'd stolen it first and ruined my masterpiece with that stupid wishing well. How was I supposed to know that everyone—my mom, my dad, even my brother—would think it was me out there and Courtney inside? How was I supposed to know my mom would grab me in the hall and say it's time to go, Courtney? I pleaded with her that I was Ali, but my mom didn't believe me, all because Courtney took my A-is-for-Ali ring when I wasn't looking. My mom yelled outside to the girl who wasn't Ali that we were leaving, and the girl who wasn't Ali turned, smiled, and said, Bye!

Off we went. Courtney got my perfect life, and I got her wrecked one. Just like that.

She ruined everything. She put her lips all over Ian Thomas. She nearly got arrested for blinding prissy Jenna Cavanaugh. She ditched Naomi and Riley, the coolest girls at school. But the very worst thing she did in my name was choose four new best friends in their place. Girls she knew I wouldn't look twice at, girls who weren't special in any way. Girls who she knew would fall all over her, desperate for the opportunity to be in her exclusive club. The girls who'd help her get everything she wanted.

Any of this sound familiar, ladies?

But don't worry. This little fairy tale can still have a happy ending for me. I saw to it that my sister paid for what she did. And now, so will you.

I tried to burn you. I tried to make you crazy. I tried to have you arrested. I've even messed with you this week— surprise! I flung myself at Aria's boyfriend. I sent poor Hanna fake tickets to a certain fashion show. I let Em believe there was a happily-ever-after for us after all. Smooch! And Spencer . . . I have a surprise for you. Look closely! It's right under your nose.

I suppose I should thank Courtney for her meticulous diary keeping. It helped me—and Mona—so much. It's all led up to this big moment. The curtain's about to go up, bitches, and the show is about to begin. Get ready to meet your maker. It won't be long now.

Kisses!

A (the real one)

No one said anything for a long moment. Aria read the note several times before it sank in. She staggered backward, awkwardly bumping into the bureau. "*Ali* wrote this? Our Ali?"

"It isn't our Ali," Spencer said in a comatose voice. "It's . . . the *real* Ali. Our Ali was . . . Courtney. The girl we knew is dead."

"No." Emily's voice was choked. "It's not possible. I don't believe it."

Suddenly, there was a snicker outside the door. Everyone shot up. Aria's skin prickled.

"Ali?" Spencer cried out.

No answer.

Aria felt for her cell phone in her pocket, but the screen still said *No Service Available.* There was no landline in this room, either. Even if they hefted the window open and yelled, this property was so remote that no one would hear.

Aria's eyes watered from the noxious odor that had permeated the room. All of a sudden, a new scent emerged. Aria's head shot up, her nostrils twitching. Emily, Hanna, and Spencer widened their eyes. They all realized what it was at the same time. That was when Aria saw white smoke billowing through the vents.

"Oh my God," she whispered, pointing. "Something's on fire."

Aria rushed to the door and pulled on the knob. She turned around fast, her face stricken. There was no need to say anything to the others—they already knew. The door was locked. They were trapped.

30

LIFE ENDS WITH A BANG, NOT A WHIMPER

The room began to fill with black, curling smoke. The temperature was slowly but steadily rising. Emily yanked at the window sash, but it didn't budge. She thought about breaking the glass, but the bedroom was in the back of the house, which was set on a steep downward slope. The jump would break their legs, if not worse.

On the other side of the room, Spencer, Aria, and Hanna were ramming their shoulders against the door, trying to break it down. When it didn't give, they collapsed in a heap on the bed, panting.

"We're going to die," Hanna whispered. "Ali's trying to kill us."

"No she's—" Emily trailed off. She was about to say that Ali wasn't—Ali *couldn't*. Billy had written that note, posing as Ali. And if he hadn't, then Melissa had. Melissa had snickered at them moments ago, laughing at everything they'd deduced. Melissa had killed Ali's sister. Melissa had set this fire. Or if not Melissa—or Billy—then someone else.

Just not Ali. Never Ali.

The air was getting so thick with smoke it was becoming hard to see. Hanna leaned over and started to cough, and Aria let out a woozy moan. Spencer ripped the top sheet from the bed and shoved it under the crack in the door to prevent more smoke from getting in, like they'd been taught in seventh-grade fire safety class. "We probably only have a few more minutes in here until the fire reaches the door," she told the others. "We have to figure out something fast."

Emily ran to the corner of the room, bumping against the closet door. Suddenly, she heard a small, thin cry. She froze. Everyone turned, hearing it, too. *Ali?* Emily thought.

But the cries were coming from somewhere very close. Then there were pounding sounds. Another cry. A muffled scream. Emily faced the closet. "Someone's *in* there!"

Spencer shot forward and turned the knob. The smell wafted out in putrid, powerful waves. Emily gagged, covering her mouth with the bottom of her shirt.

"Oh my God," Spencer shouted. Then Emily looked down and screamed louder than she'd ever screamed before. A rotted corpse was splayed out in the bottom of the almost-empty closet. The legs were bent halfway up the wall at a disfiguring angle, and the head lolled off to the left, resting on top of an Adidas shoe box.

The skin was a sallow yellow, and there was a horrible waxy substance on what was left of the cheeks. The skin and muscles around the mouth had rotted away into a hollow pit. The beautiful golden hair looked like a wig, and the forehead swarmed with maggots.

It was Ian Thomas.

Emily kept screaming and shut her eyes, but the image seemed branded on the back of her eyelids. Then, something shot forward and touched her foot. She shot back and tried to slam the door. "Stop!" Spencer screamed. "Emily, wait!"

Emily froze, whimpering. Spencer pushed around her and pulled another body from the closet, someone who'd almost been crushed by Ian's body. Emily gasped. It was a girl, her mouth gagged. *Melissa.* Her blue eyes stared at them imploringly.

Everyone helped to untie the thick ropes around her wrists and ankles and pull the duct tape from her mouth. Melissa immediately doubled over and began to cough. Tears streamed down her face. She collapsed into Spencer, her sobs tortured and terrified. "Are you okay?" Spencer cried.

"She kidnapped me and threw me in the trunk of the car," Melissa coughed. "I woke up a couple times, but she kept drugging me to knock me out. And when I woke up again, I was in . . . " She trailed off, her eyes sliding to the half-opened closet. Her face contorted with pain.

Then, Melissa sniffed the air. The smoke was pouring

into the room so fast, a fine gray haze had begun to swirl. Melissa began to shake. "We're all going to die."

Everyone rushed to the center of the room and held one another. Emily shivered uncontrollably. She could feel someone's heart beating against hers. "It'll be okay," Spencer repeated over and over in Melissa's ear. "We need to find a way out of here."

"There *is* no way!" Melissa's eyes were full of tears. "Don't you see?"

"Wait a minute." Aria leaped to her feet. She looked around the room quizzically, her forehead furrowed. "I think this is the room with the passage that leads to the kitchen."

"What are you talking about?" Hanna asked.

"Don't you remember?" Aria cried. "We hid in here to scare Jason."

Aria marched to the dresser and shoved it out of the way. To Emily's astonishment, there was the small door, about the height of a golden retriever. Aria pulled the latch and kicked it open, revealing a dark tunnel. Melissa gasped.

"Come on," Spencer urged, sinking to her hands and knees and squeezing through the tiny door. She dragged her sister through after her. Aria went next, then Hanna. Emily's stomach jumped. The tunnel smelled like Ian's rotting body.

"Emily!" Spencer's echoing voice sounded very far away. "Hurry!"

Emily took a deep breath, folded her shoulders, and crawled inside. The tunnel was about ten feet long and let out in a small, closet-size room that looked as though it had been closed up for years. There were piles of dust and tons of dead bugs in the corners and a big water stain on the ceiling. Aria tried the knob to the far door that led to the rickety wooden staircase, but it didn't budge. "It's jammed," she whispered.

"It can't be," Spencer insisted. She threw her shoulder against it in desperation. Emily, Aria, and Hanna joined in. Finally, the wood splintered, then gave way. Emily let out a relieved sound that was a mix between a sigh and a wail.

They scampered down the stairs and opened a third door. The heat rushed at them, stinging their eyes and skin. The room was filled with even thicker plumes of smoke. Emily fumbled around the kitchen island, trying to get her bearings. She staggered in the direction of the front door. A shadow moved to her left, in and out of the noxious fog. Someone was hammering the windows shut so there was no chance of getting out.

Emily froze when she saw the blond hair, the heart-shaped face, the kissable lips. *Ali.*

Ali wheeled around and stared at Emily as if she'd seen a ghost. The hammer fell clumsily to the floor. Her eyes were slate gray and cold, her mouth misshaped into a half smirk. A sob rose in Emily's chest. All of a sudden, she knew that this girl had written that note . . . and that everything in it was true. Her heart broke into a million pieces.

Ali turned and raced for the door just as Emily shot forward, grabbing Ali by the arm and spinning her around. Ali's mouth made a startled *O*. Emily held her roughly by the shoulders, her grip strong.

"How could you do this?" Emily demanded.

Ali tried to wrench free. Her eyes seethed with loathing. "I already told you," she rasped. "You bitches ruined my life." It didn't even sound like her voice.

"But . . . I *loved* you," Emily squeaked, her eyes filling with tears.

Ali let out a perverse giggle. "You are *such* a loser, Emily."

It felt like she'd driven a long skewer straight through Emily's heart. She squeezed Ali's shoulders hard, wanting her to know how much it hurt. *How can you say that?* she was about to scream. *How can you hate us so much?*

But then a giant boom filled the air, momentarily blinding her. There was a bright white light and a rush of heat. Emily covered her head and eyes as the force of the explosion lifted her off the ground. She felt a *snap*, then a *crash*. She landed hard on her shoulder, her teeth clanging together.

The world was white for a moment. Calm. Empty. When Emily opened her eyes again, the sound and heat and pain rushed back in. She was lying near the front door, a pool of blood by her mouth. Desperate, she fumbled for the doorknob. It burned to the touch, but it turned. She crawled to the porch and then to the lawn, sprawling on the cold, wet grass.

When Emily opened her eyes again, someone was coughing next to her. Spencer and her sister were collapsed on the grass nearby. Aria was by the big chestnut tree, crumpled on her side. Hanna was near the driveway, slowly pushing herself to a sitting position.

Emily gazed back at the big house. Smoke billowed from every crack. Flames leaped from the roof. A shadow passed in front of the living room window. And then there was a thunderous cracking sound, and the whole house exploded.

Emily shrieked, covered her eyes, and curled into a ball. *Just count to a hundred,* she told herself. *Just pretend you're swimming laps. Just keep your eyes shut until this is over.* The air felt hot and dirty, and the sound was louder than a thousand airplanes taking off. A couple of sparks rained down onto Emily's shoulders, hot snaps against her skin.

The explosions continued for a few long seconds more. When they subsided, Emily parted her fingers and peered out from beneath her hands. The house was nothing but a giant mountain of fire.

"Ali," she whispered, but the word was immediately swallowed up as the chimney crashed to the ground. Ali was still inside.

31

THE REMAINING PIECES

Spencer lay coughing on the lawn a safe distance away from the house, Melissa out cold next to her. The structure burned steadily, an inferno of yellow and orange. Every so often, a mini explosion spit sparks high into the sky. The upstairs level, where they'd recently been imprisoned, was nothing but a brittle, blazing carcass.

The other girls crawled over to them. "Is everyone okay?" Spencer shouted. Emily nodded. Hanna coughed out a yes. Aria had her face in her hands, but weakly said she was fine. A sharp wind whipped around their faces. It was heavy with the odor of charred wood and dead bodies.

"I can't get that letter out of my head," Emily said in a monotone, shivering in her thin sweater. "Ali was so angry at her sister for switching places and sending her away she *killed* her."

"Yep," Spencer said, shifting her weight on the bumpy ground.

"Ian had nothing to do with it. Billy didn't, either. Ali

just needed to pin it on someone. And then she was going to kill us." It was like Emily needed to say all of this out loud to convince herself that it had really happened.

"It was Courtney who talked to us when we tried to steal her Time Capsule flag. It was the only way to make her parents think she was the sane twin . . ." Aria said in equal disbelief, wiping soot from her face. "And Courtney picked us at the charity drive because she *had* to—she couldn't be friends with Naomi and Riley anymore. She didn't know them—she only knew us."

"Naomi and Riley told me Ali ditched them for no reason at all," Hanna sighed.

Spencer hugged her knees. Another spark rose high in the air. A terrified squirrel skittered down a nearby tree and took off across the lawn. "When Ian came to my porch, he said he was on the verge of figuring out a crazy secret that would turn Rosewood upside-down. He must have known that Courtney had been home that weekend."

"And Ali must have known we'd think Jason or Wilden set that fire," Hanna wailed. "Except the fire didn't go as planned—she got hurt. So she called Wilden, and he whisked her away, thinking she was following her parents' orders to stay hidden. But really, she left to make us look crazier."

"And I guess Ali put those pictures on Billy's laptop," Spencer continued, wincing as something else inside the house popped and crackled. She checked on Melissa, who held her face in her hands, quietly sobbing. "She was also the one who'd called the cops and tipped them off, saying Billy killed Jenna."

"But *she* killed Jenna," Aria said.

Everyone fell silent. Spencer shut her eyes, trying to imagine Ali taking beautiful, shy, *blind* Jenna Cavanaugh and throwing her into that ditch. It was too horrible to comprehend.

"Remember that picture A sent Emily of Ali, Courtney, and Jenna together?" Spencer said after a moment. "Jenna was the only person besides Ali's family and Wilden who knew there were twins. Maybe Jenna suspected the first switch. She met Courtney the same weekend it happened." She cocked her head. "But why would Ali send us that photo if she didn't want us to know what Jenna knew?"

"Because she could," Hanna answered. "Maybe she banked on Jenna never saying anything. And then when it seemed like Jenna *might*, she . . ." She trailed off, burying her face in her hands. "You know."

Melissa lifted up her face with a groan. It was covered with thick stripes of ash and dirt. There was a gash on her shoulder and rope burns on her hands and feet. She smelled like Ian's rotting flesh. Queasiness roiled in Spencer's gut.

Spencer reached out to clean a streak of ash from her sister's hair. Her eyes filled with tears. She couldn't believe how wrong she'd been about Melissa. How wrong they'd *all* been. "Why did Ali want to hurt you?"

Melissa propped herself up, shielding her eyes from the bright flames. She coughed, then cleared her throat. "When Jason told me about the twins years ago, he said that Ali and Courtney had no contact whatsoever—that they hated each other." She gingerly stretched her neck and rolled her shoulders. "So when you told me that Courtney said Ali told her lots of stuff about you guys, I got suspicious."

There was a *crack* from inside the house, and the girls instinctively turned away. Part of the second floor collapsed to the ground with a groan. "I talked to Wilden," Melissa said over the noise. "He said they were a little worried about Courtney when she first came home from the hospital, especially after you guys said you saw Ian's body. Jason wondered if Courtney had killed Ian in revenge for him killing Ali."

"She did murder him." Aria pushed a twig into the soggy dirt. "Though not for revenge."

The big glass windowpanes in the DiLaurentises' sunroom popped and shattered. Glass rained onto the lawn, and the girls covered their heads.

"But Courtney had an alibi for that night," Melissa went on, brushing a piece of blood-soaked hair from her eyes. "And then Billy came along, and suddenly everything seemed to make sense."

Aria huddled closer to Hanna.

"But when Courtney showed up," Melissa said, pulling the sleeves of her filthy cashmere sweater over her hands,

"I couldn't stop thinking about all the inconsistencies in Billy's case."

· The fire crackled for a few moments. Something crashed from behind the house. Emily flinched, and Spencer grabbed her hand.

"I followed Courtney . . . Ali . . . a lot," Melissa admitted. "It wasn't until I went to the Preserve that I knew for sure what had happened."

Spencer's mouth dropped open. The pamphlet of the Preserve she'd seen in Melissa's room. The appointment with the therapist. "So *that's* why you went there?"

A stream of sparks erupted from the top of the house, into the air. "I talked to Ali's old roommate, Iris," Melissa said. "And she knew everything—even that you were going to be her roommate, Hanna."

"Oh God," Hanna moaned, her shoulders going limp.

Spencer placed her palms on the top of her head. They'd missed so many clues. Ali had set a brilliant trap . . . and they'd walked right into it. She looked at her sister. "Why didn't you tell me this stuff about the Preserve earlier?"

"I only went there this morning." White steam emerged from Melissa's mouth. It was getting colder out by the second. "I was on my way to the police station afterward, but someone jumped me in the parking lot. When I woke up, I was in the trunk. I recognized Ali's voice."

Spencer stared blankly as the old teak swing set behind the house caught fire. Ali must have grabbed Melissa after she came over to Spencer's to get ready for the dance. She never should have told Ali that Melissa had warned Spencer to keep her distance. . . .

Then another thought struck her. "Did you say Ali threw you into the trunk of her car?"

Melissa nodded, loosening a dry, charred leaf from her matted blond hair.

"You were there on our drive up here," Spencer gasped, the knobs of her spine pressing into the rough trunk of the tree. "You were with us the whole time."

"I *knew* I heard something," Aria whispered.

They were silent for a few moments, staring dazedly at the house. The fire crackled and hissed. Far off, another sound emerged. It sounded like sirens.

Melissa struggled to stand, still leaning against the big tree. "Can I see the note she wrote you?"

Spencer reached into her hoodie, searching for the letter, but the pockets were empty. She looked at Emily. "Do you have it?"

Emily shook her head. Aria and Hanna looked clueless, too.

Everyone turned to the ruined house. If the note had slipped out of Spencer's hands, it was nothing but ash now.

Just then, a fire truck screamed up the driveway. Three firemen jumped out and began to unroll the hoses into the lake. A fourth fireman ran to the girls. "Are you okay?" He immediately radioed for an ambulance and the police. "How did this happen?"

Spencer looked at the others. "Someone tried to kill us," she said. And then she burst into tears.

"Spence," Emily said, touching Spencer's shoulder.

"It's okay," Aria cooed. Hanna hugged her, too, and so did Melissa.

But Spencer couldn't stop crying. How had they not suspected Ali was behind this? How had they been so blind? Ali had said a lot of the right things, too—exactly what they all wanted to hear: *I missed you guys. I'm so sorry. I want things to change.* She'd told Spencer *you're the sister I've always wanted.* Spencer was putty in her hands. They all were . . . and they'd all almost died for it.

The fireman slid his walkie-talkie back into his pocket, and the girls broke apart. "The ambulance is on its way," he said, and beckoned for the girls to follow him.

As they climbed the slope, moving farther from the house, Spencer poked her sister's arm. "You *had* to figure this out before me, didn't you?" she teased, wiping away tears. Leave it to Melissa to one-up her even with *this.*

Melissa blushed. "I'm just glad you're okay."

"I'm glad *you're* okay," Spencer said back.

The smoldering house loomed in the distance. Beds and chairs and dressers crashed through the brittle flooring to the first level, sending up fiery plumes. Emily stared hard at the flames as if searching for something. Spencer touched her arm. "You okay?"

Emily pulled her bottom lip into her mouth. She

glanced at the fireman. "There was someone in the house when it exploded. Is there any chance she's . . . ?"

The fireman stared at the remains of the house and scratched his stubbly chin. He shook his head gravely. "No one could have survived that fire. I'm sorry, girls, but she's gone."

32

HANNA MARIN, TRULY FABULOUS

"Here we go." Hanna plunked down a stiff cardboard holder of four hot coffees on the café table. "One skim cappuccino, one regular latte, and one café au lait with soy milk."

"Sweet," Aria said, grabbing a packet of Sugar In The Raw. She tore it open with her neon-yellow-painted nails. Aria kept telling Hanna and the others that neon yellow was *the* hottest color in Europe, but no one had been brave enough to try it yet.

"It's about time," Spencer grumbled, taking a greedy sip of her cappuccino. She'd been cramming for the big AP econ pre-exam all week and had just pulled an all-nighter.

"Thanks, Hanna." Emily adjusted her pleated Free People top. Hanna had *finally* gotten her to stop wearing swimming tees under her Rosewood Day blazer.

Hanna sat down and gazed around the table at Spencer's stacks of AP econ textbooks and notes, Aria's iPod, probably full of weird Scandinavian yodeling bands, and Emily's palmistry book, which promised to teach anyone how to tell fortunes. It was just like old times . . . only better.

A news bulletin flashed on the plasma TV on Steam's back wall. A familiar reporter stood in front of an even more familiar pile of rubble. *Police still searching through DiLaurentis rubble,* the caption said. Hanna touched Aria's arm.

"Recovery workers are still sifting through the burned wreckage of the house that once belonged to Alison DiLaurentis's family, searching for the *real* Alison's remains," the blond reporter shouted over the sound of heavy machinery. "But they're saying it'll be weeks before they can be sure Alison died in the fire."

The fireman who'd rescued them the night of the fire appeared on the screen. "I was there moments after the house exploded," he said. "It's very possible Alison's body incinerated instantly."

"As usual, the DiLaurentis family cannot be reached for comment," the reporter added.

The broadcast cut to a commercial for All That Jazz, the Broadway musical–themed restaurant at the King James Mall. Hanna and her friends sipped in silence, staring out at the lawn. The snow had finally melted, and a couple of overeager daffodils had sprouted in the beds near the flagpole.

Five weeks had passed since Ali almost killed them. As soon as they got home from the Poconos, Wilden and the other Rosewood PD detectives had opened an official investigation into Ali. Her house of cards collapsed ridiculously fast: Police found copies of A's notes to the girls on a cell phone underneath the deck behind the DiLaurentises' new house. They'd discovered that the laptop found in Billy's truck had been tampered with. They analyzed the Polaroids Aria had found in the woods and determined that the reflection in the windows was one of the DiLaurentis sisters. It was unclear why Ali had taken the photos—except that she was obsessed with the life her sister had stolen from her—but she must have buried the photos shortly after pushing her sister in the hole, ridding herself of the evidence.

There was some talk of arresting the DiLaurentis family as accessories to Ali's crimes, but Mr. and Mrs. DiLaurentis and even Jason had fled the area without a trace. Hanna took another sip of her coffee, letting the hot liquid wash over her tongue. Had they suspected all along that one sister had killed the other? Was that why they'd quickly whisked her back to the mental hospital after the girl everyone thought was Ali went missing? Or had Mr. and Mrs. DiLaurentis vanished simply out of shame and horror that their beautiful, perfect daughter had done such barbaric things?

As for Hanna and the others, the Ali aftermath had been insane. Reporters banged on their doors at all hours of the night. The girls traveled to New York for an interview on the *Today* show and did a photo shoot in *People*. They attended a society-studded gala concert sponsored by the Philadelphia Orchestra to raise money for Jenna's Seeing Eye Dogs Fund and a new scholarship set up in Ian Thomas's name. But things had just begun to calm down, and life had almost returned to semi-normal.

Hanna tried not to think about what had happened with Ali, but that was like asking her to go a whole day not counting calories—pointless. All this time, Hanna had thought Ali had chosen her because she'd seen some special spark in Hanna that simply needed to be nurtured and encouraged. But she'd befriended her for the exact opposite reasons. Hanna had been *un*special. A joke. A ploy for revenge. The only saving grace was that Ali had done this to *all* of them, not only her. And now that Hanna knew both sisters were crazy, would she really have wanted to be singled out by either of them?

Aria tipped back her coffee cup so far that Hanna could see the recycled paper mark on the bottom. "So when are the movers coming?"

Hanna straightened up. "Tomorrow."

"You must be thrilled." Spencer tied her hair back in a loose ponytail.

"You don't know the half of it."

That was the other big news: A few days after Ali nearly killed them, Hanna had received a call while she was lounging in bed watching *Oprah*. "I'm at the Philadelphia airport," her mother barked on the other end. "I'll see you in about an hour."

"*What?*" Hanna squawked, startling Dot from his Burberry doggie bed. "Why?"

Ms. Marin had asked for a transfer back to the ad agency's Philadelphia office. "Ever since you called me about those fashion show tickets, I've been worried about you," she explained. "So I spoke to your father. Why didn't you tell me he sent you to a *mental hospital*, Hanna?"

Hanna hadn't known how to answer—it wasn't exactly something she could've written in an e-mail or on the back of a *Greetings from Rosewood!* postcard. And anyway, she'd figured her mom already knew. Didn't they get *People* in Singapore?

"It's absolutely deplorable!" Ms. Marin ranted. "What was he thinking? Or maybe he wasn't thinking at all. All he cares about is that *woman* and her daughter."

Hanna sniffed and there was static on the line. Ms. Marin said, "I'm moving back in, but things need to change between us. No more relaxed rules. No more me looking the other way. You need to have a curfew and boundaries, and we need to talk about things. Like if someone tries to institutionalize you. Or if a crazy friend tries to kill you. Okay?"

A lump formed in Hanna's throat. "Okay." For once in her life, her mom had said exactly what Hanna needed her to say.

Everything after that happened so fast. There were arguments, bartering, and crying—on Kate's and Isabel's parts—but Hanna's mom was firm. She was staying,

Hanna was staying, and Tom, Isabel, and Kate had to go. The house-hunting started that weekend, but apparently Kate went total diva and thumbs-downed every property they looked at. Because the process was taking so long, they were going to have to move into a townhouse in East Hollis, the most hippie-ish, unkempt district of Rosewood while they continued to look.

A flash of blond hair caught Hanna's eye across the café. Naomi, Riley, and Kate strutted in, settled into one of the tables nearest the door, and gave Hanna a nasty smirk. *Loser,* Naomi mouthed. *Bitch,* Riley seconded.

Not that Hanna really cared. More than a month had passed since Hanna lost her queen bee status, and all the things she'd most feared hadn't happened. She hadn't spontaneously gained back the weight she'd lost. She hadn't sprouted volcanic zits. She hadn't woken up to find her teeth were snaggled and crooked. In fact, she'd lost a couple pounds, not having to binge fretfully whenever some other girl stole away a bit of her power. Her skin glowed, and her hair shone. Guys from other prep schools still ogled her at Rive Gauche, and Sasha at Otter still held clothes for her. Cheesy as it was, Hanna had begun to wonder if it wasn't popularity that made her truly beautiful but something much deeper. Maybe she really *was* fabulous Hanna Marin, after all.

The end-of-the-day bell rang, and everyone emerged from the classrooms. Hanna's stomach clenched as she noticed a tall, black-haired boy walking by himself toward the art wing. Mike.

She rolled her half-empty coffee cup between her hands, stood, and started across the café.

"Going to see the school counselor, Psycho?" Kate teased as she passed.

Mike watched Hanna as she approached. His black hair was mussed, and there was a cute, uncertain smile on his face. Before he could say a word, Hanna marched right up to him and kissed him on the mouth. She wrapped her arms around him, and Mike quickly did the same. Someone hooted.

Hanna and Mike broke apart, breathing hard. Mike looked into her eyes. "Uh . . . hi!"

"Hi, yourself," Hanna whispered.

The day Hanna returned to Rosewood from the Poconos, she'd driven straight to the Montgomery home and begged Mike to take her back. Thankfully, Mike forgave Hanna for dumping him—although he'd added, "You have to make it up to me. I think I deserve a couple of stripteases, right?"

She leaned in to kiss Mike again when his cell phone bleated in his pocket. "Hold that thought," he said, putting the phone to his ear without saying hello. "Okay," he said a couple of times. When he hung up, his face was pale.

"What is it?" Hanna asked.

Mike glanced across the café to Aria. "That was Dad," he called to her. "Meredith's in labor."

33

ARIA MONTGOMERY, TYPICAL ROSEWOOD KOOK

Aria had begged her old friends to come with her to Rosewood Memorial Hospital, and now the four of them and Mike sat in the waiting room outside Labor and Delivery. An hour had passed since they'd heard anything, and they'd read the waiting room's entire stash of *Glamour*, *Vogue*, *Car & Driver*, and *Good Housekeeping*, and had downloaded about a hundred iPhone apps. Byron was holed up in the delivery room, doing his I'm-going-to-be-a-father-again thing. It was beyond bizarre to see her dad so gung-ho about the birthing. Apparently, when both Aria and Mike were born, Byron had fainted at the first sight of blood and had to spend the rest of the evening in the ER getting IV fluids to keep his blood pressure up.

Aria stared across the room at a nondescript painting of a desert vista and sighed.

"You okay?" Emily asked.

"Yeah," Aria answered. "Except I think my butt's asleep."

Emily gave Aria a concerned look. But Aria was pretty sure she *was* okay about all of this, unconventional as it was. The day after Ali had tried to kill them, Aria had gotten a call on her cell phone from her mom. Ella was in tears, devastated that something awful had almost happened to Aria.

Aria had admitted why she'd stayed away, that she'd wanted to give Ella a chance to be happy with Xavier. Ella had breathed out and cried, "That scumbag! Aria, you should have *told* me immediately."

Ella promptly broke up with Xavier and things between Aria and her mother slowly returned to normal. Now Aria was back to spending half her time at Ella's, half her time at Byron and Meredith's. She and Ella had even talked a little about the impending new baby. Although Ella seemed a little sad about it, she also said it was the way life went. "Most things don't work out the way you want them to," she said. Aria knew *that* all too well. Practically the only thing she'd learned from the Ali experience was that some things were too good to be true.

Including Ali herself.

Byron pushed through the waiting room door. He wore blue scrubs, a face mask, and one of those weird anti-germ shower caps. "It's a girl," he said breathlessly.

Everyone jumped up. "Can we see her?" Aria asked, slinging her yak-fur bag over her shoulder.

Byron nodded and led them down the quiet hallway until they came to a room with a big window. Meredith sat propped up in bed. Her hair was matted to her head, but her skin glowed. In her arms was a tiny pink bundle.

Aria stepped inside and gazed at the little creature. The girl's eyes were little slits, her nose was nothing more than a button, and she wore a preppy-looking pink cap on her head. *Ugh*. Aria would definitely have to knit her something cooler.

"Do you want to hold your sister?" Meredith asked.

Sister.

Aria approached tentatively. Meredith smiled and placed the newborn in Aria's arms. She felt warm and smelled of powder. "She's beautiful," Aria whispered. Behind her, Hanna sighed with pleasure. Spencer and Emily made cooing noises. Mike looked flabbergasted.

"What are you going to name her?" Aria asked.

"We haven't decided." Meredith pursed her lips bashfully. "We thought you might like to help us choose."

"Really?" Aria breathed, touched. Meredith nodded.

A nurse knocked on the door. "How are we all doing?" Aria gave the baby to the nurse, who pressed a stethoscope to her tiny chest.

"We should go," Spencer said, giving Aria a hug. Hanna and Emily piled on, too. They used to do mass hugs like this back in sixth and seventh grades, especially after something huge had happened. Of course, there used to be a fifth girl in the mass hugs, but Aria decided not to dwell on Ali. She didn't want her to ruin the moment.

After her friends disappeared through the double doors—Mike hand-in-hand with Hanna—Aria returned to the waiting room and slumped down on the couch nearest the TV. Predictably, the news was droning on about how Ali's body still hadn't been found in the wreckage in the Poconos. A reporter was interviewing a leather-faced woman in Kansas who'd started a Facebook group claiming that Ali was still alive. "Don't you people think it's strange you haven't found even *one* of her teeth or bones in that fire?" the woman cackled, her eyes round and crazed. "Alison is alive. Mark my words."

Aria stabbed at the remote to change the channel. There was no way Ali was still out there. She'd gone down with that house and that was that.

"Aria?" said a voice.

Aria looked up. "Oh," she said weakly, rising to her feet. Her heart started to thump. "H-hi."

Noel Kahn stood in the doorway, wearing a beat-up black T-shirt and effortlessly fitting jeans. Aria could smell his skin from across the room, a blend of soap and spices. They'd barely spoken since the Valentine's Day dance, and Aria had figured things with him were ruined for good.

Noel crossed the room and sat down on one of the lumpy chairs. "Mike texted me about your sister. Congratulations."

"Thanks," Aria said. Her muscles seemed hardened in place, like clay after it had been fired.

A bunch of doctors in blue scrubs walked past the waiting room, their stethoscopes jostling against their chests. Noel stuck his finger into a tiny hole in the knee of his jeans. "I don't know if this matters, but I didn't kiss Courtney. *Ali.* Whoever she was. She kissed me."

Aria nodded, a lump in her throat. As soon as Ali had made her motives clear, it was painfully obvious what had happened. Ali had been desperate to get Aria to the Poconos, not because she wanted to be friends with Aria but because she wanted all the girls together so she could kill them in one fell swoop.

"I know," Aria answered, staring at the toy box in the corner of the waiting room. It was filled with dog-eared picture books, ugly, yarn-haired dolls, and mismatched Legos. "I'm really sorry. I should have trusted you."

"I've missed you," Noel said quietly.

Aria dared to look up. "I missed you, too."

Ever so slowly, Noel rose from his chair and sat down next to her. "For the record, you're the most beautiful, interesting person I've ever met. I've always thought that, even in seventh grade."

"You liar." Aria half smiled.

"I would never lie about something like that," Noel said sternly.

And then he leaned forward and kissed her.

34

SPENCER HASTINGS'S BEAUTIFUL, IMPERFECT LIFE

Andrew Campbell picked up Spencer from the hospital in his Mini Cooper and drove her home. KYW news was running the same report about how the police still hadn't found any evidence of Ali's body in the rubble.

Spencer pressed her forehead to the window and shut her eyes.

Andrew pulled up to Spencer's curb and shifted the Mini into park. "You okay?"

"I need a minute," Spencer mumbled.

At first glance, her street was resplendent and picturesque, all the houses grand and impressive, all the yards fenced in and maintained, and all the driveways paved with bluestone or brick. But if Spencer looked closer, the imperfections were obvious. The Cavanaugh house had been dark since Jenna's death, a FOR SALE sign on the front lawn. The oak where Toby's tree house had once stood was now a rotted stump. The hole where Jenna's body had been found was filled in with thick, black dirt. The Jenna shrine remained at the curb, so swollen that it encompassed some of the neighbor's curb and yard. The Ali shrine, on the other hand, had been dismantled. Spencer had no idea what happened to all the photos and stuffed animals and candles—they'd disappeared overnight. No one wanted to memorialize Alison DiLaurentis anymore. She was no longer Rosewood's blameless, beautiful darling.

Spencer stared at the big Victorian on the corner of the cul-de-sac. *You're Spencer, right?* Ali had asked Spencer the day she'd sneaked into the DiLaurentis yard to steal Ali's piece of the Time Capsule flag. Spencer had thought Ali was only pretending not to know who Spencer was . . . but she actually *didn't* have a clue. Courtney had to learn everything about Ali's life—fast.

Spencer could also see the dilapidated barn at the back of her house, forever ruined by the fire Ali had started. *I tried to burn you. I tried to have you arrested. And now, here we are.* The night Ali went missing, when Spencer and Ali got in that awful fight, the Ali she knew stormed out, probably on her way to meet Ian. The real Ali, the one whose life had been stolen, was waiting for her.

I saw two blondes in the woods, Ian had told Spencer on the back porch before his trial. Spencer had seen those blondes, too. At first she'd assumed it was Ian or maybe Jason or Billy, but in the end, it had been two identical sisters. Of course the real Ali knew when the hole was going to be filled with concrete—she'd probably heard her parents talking about it when they'd picked her up from the hospital that weekend. She'd known how deep the hole was, too, and how hard she'd have to shove her sister to kill her. Ali probably thought that after the deed was done, she'd go back into the house and reclaim her life. Except that hadn't happened.

Spencer still had nightmares about those last moments in the Poconos before the house erupted into flames. One minute, Ali and Emily were grappling by the door. The next, the house was filled with a white fireball . . . and Ali was gone. Had she been blown into another room? Had they unknowingly stumbled over her dead body while trying to escape? Spencer had seen the kooks on the news who theorized that Ali was still alive. "It makes perfect sense," a wild-haired man told Larry King last week. "The DiLaurentis parents *vanished*. They obviously caught up with their daughter and are hiding in another country."

But Spencer didn't believe it. Ali had perished with the house, Ian's body, and her terrifying letter. *Finis. Finito.* The end.

Spencer turned back to Andrew, letting out a held breath. "It's all so . . . sad." She gestured out the window to her street. "I used to love living here. I thought it was perfect. But now it's . . . ruined. There are so many terrible memories here."

"We'll have to make good memories to override the bad ones," Andrew assured her. But Spencer wasn't convinced that anything could really do that.

There was a knock on the window, and Spencer jumped. Melissa peered in. "Hey, Spence. Can you come inside?"

There was a look on her face that made Spencer think something had happened, and Spencer's stomach flipped with worry. Andrew leaned over and kissed Spencer on the forehead. "Call me later."

Spencer followed Melissa across the lawn, admiring her sister's soft red cashmere V-neck sweater and black skinny jeans. She'd helped Melissa pick them out from Otter—Melissa had actually listened to Spencer when she told Melissa that she was dressing like a clone of their mother. It was one of the few good things that had come out of this nightmare—Spencer and Melissa were finally getting along for real. No more competitiveness. No more nasty comments. Surviving that fire—escaping their half sister—had put everything in perspective. So far, anyway.

The house smelled comfortingly like tomato sauce and garlic. For the first time in two months, the living room was spotless, the floors looked waxed, and all the oil paintings in the halls hung straight and even. When Spencer peered into the dining room, she saw that the table was set. Perrier sparkled in water glasses. A bottle of wine was airing in a decanter on the rolling bar cart.

"What's going on?" Spencer murmured uneasily. It was highly doubtful her mom was entertaining.

"Spence?"

Mr. Hastings appeared in the kitchen doorway, dressed in a gray suit from work. Spencer had barely seen him since the night she exposed the affair. Stunningly, Mrs. Hastings appeared behind him, a tired but content smile on her face. "Dinner's ready," she chirped, removing an oven mitt from her right hand.

"O-okay," Spencer stammered. She walked into the dining room, still staring at them. Were they seriously going to pretend that nothing had happened? Could they really brush this under the rug? Did Spencer even want them to?

Mr. Hastings poured Spencer a tiny sip of wine and gave Melissa a regular-size glass. He bustled around with Spencer's mom, carrying bowls and spoons and a basket of garlic bread to the table. Spencer and Melissa exchanged an uneasy glance. He *never* helped with dinner preparations, usually sitting at the table like a king while Mrs. Hastings did all the work.

Everyone sat down, Spencer's parents on either end of the table, Spencer and Melissa on opposite sides. The room was very quiet. Steam rose from the bowl of pasta puttanesca. The smell of garlic and spicy wine tickled Spencer's nose. The family stared at one another like they were strangers forced to sit together on an airplane. Finally, Mr. Hastings cleared his throat.

"Want to play Star Power?" he said.

Spencer's mouth dropped open. Melissa's, too. Mrs. Hastings let out a weary laugh. "He's kidding, girls."

Mr. Hastings rested his palms on the table. "This talk is long overdue." He paused to sip his wine. "I need to tell you that I never meant to hurt you. *Any* of you. But I did. That's not going to change, and I'm not going to ask you to forgive me. But I want you to know that whatever happens, I'll be there for all of you. Things are different now, and they'll never go back to being the way they were, but please know that every day, I feel terrible about what I did. I've felt terrible about it since it happened. And I feel terrible that someone we're related to did something horrible to both of you. I would have never forgiven myself if something had happened." He let out a small sniffle.

Spencer rocked her fork back and forth on the table, not sure what to say. It always made her nervous and uncomfortable to see her dad get emotional—and this was the first time he'd even hinted at being Ali's real father. She wanted to tell her dad that it was okay—she forgave him, and it was best forgotten. But she was pretty sure that would be a lie.

"So what's going to happen?" Melissa asked in a small voice, kneading the cloth napkin next to her plate.

Mrs. Hastings took a tiny sip of sparkling water. "We're working on things, just trying to understand what happened."

"Are you getting back together?" Spencer blurted.

"Right now, no," Mrs. Hastings explained. "Your dad's renting a townhouse closer to the city. But we'll see how it goes."

"We'll have to take it one day at a time," Mr. Hastings said, rolling up the sleeves of his button-down. "But we want to try to meet for dinner here at least once a week. To talk to you together and hang out. So . . . here we are." He reached across the table, grabbed a piece of garlic bread, and bit off a piece with a loud *crunch*.

And so they went on, not talking about Star Power achievements, not out-bragging one another, not making insidious little insults disguised as compliments. Finally, it occurred to Spencer what was going on. They were being . . . *normal*. This was probably what most families did at dinner every day.

Spencer coiled a piece of pasta around her fork and took a big, sloppy bite. Okay, so maybe this wasn't the family she'd always dreamed of. Maybe her parents wouldn't get back together in the end, and her dad would remain in his rented townhouse or move to a house of his own. But if they could talk about things—if they were really *interested* in one another—then that was a change for the better.

As Mrs. Hastings brought in pints of Ben & Jerry's and four spoons, Melissa tapped Spencer's foot under the table. "Want to stay with me in the townhouse in Philly for the weekend?" she whispered. "Tons more cool clubs and restaurants have opened up."

"Really?" Spencer asked. Melissa had never invited her to the townhouse before.

"Yep." Melissa nodded. "There's a guest room for you. *And* I'll even let you reorganize my bookshelf." She winked. "Maybe you can file the books by color and size instead of in alphabetical order."

"You've got a deal," Spencer said, giggling.

Two bright pink spots appeared on Melissa's cheeks, almost like she was happy. The warm feeling in Spencer's stomach grew and grew. Just a few weeks ago, she'd had two sisters. Now she was down to only one. But maybe Melissa was the only sister she'd ever really needed. Perhaps Melissa even could be the sister Spencer had always wanted . . . and Spencer could be that sister to Melissa, too. Maybe all they had to do was give each other a chance.

35

EMILY FIELDS PUTS IT ALL TO REST

Instead of driving straight home from the hospital, Emily made the turn down Goshen Road. It was a hilly, picturesque lane that featured a series of dairy farms, a crumbling stone wall from the Revolutionary War, and a mansion so huge and sprawling that it had three separate garages and its own helipad.

Eventually, she came to the wrought-iron gate of St. Basil's cemetery. Dusk was setting in fast, but the gate was still open, and there were a couple of cars parked in the lot. Emily pulled in next to a Jeep Liberty and turned off the engine. She sat for a moment, taking heaping breaths. Then she reached into the glove compartment and pulled out a plastic bag she'd stashed there.

Her Vans sank in the wet, soft grass as she walked past the graves, many of them bearing fresh flowers and American flags. Emily reached the headstone she was looking for in no time, wedged prettily between two pine trees. *Alison Lauren DiLaurentis,* the grave said. It was surprising that it was still here, being that Ali's family had left Rosewood forever.

And that it wasn't actually Ali who was buried here, but Courtney.

Emily traced the *A* on the headstone with her thumb. She had prided herself on knowing Ali so intimately, better than any of the others. And yet she hadn't known that the girl she was kissing wasn't the Ali she'd known all those years before. She'd been too blinded by love. Even today, a big part of her still couldn't believe it had happened. She couldn't grasp that the girl who'd come back to them wasn't the Ali she'd known—and that the Ali she'd known wasn't the real Ali at all.

Emily knelt down next to Ali's grave and plunged her hand into the plastic bag. The patent leather change purse squeaked against her fingers. She'd stuffed it with as many photos and notes from Ali as she could, the sides bulging and the zipper barely closing. Sighing, she traced a finger over the *E*. Ali had presented it to Emily after French class in sixth grade. "*Pour vous*, from *moi*," she'd said.

"What's the occasion?" Emily asked.

"There isn't one." Ali bumped Emily's hip. "Just that I hope Emily Fields is my very bestest friend forever."

Emily could practically hear Ali's voice now, whistling in the wind. She started to dig into the earth next to the grave. Dirt got underneath her fingernails and all over her palms, but she burrowed down at least a foot before she stopped. Taking a deep breath, she dropped the change purse in. Hopefully, the purse would stay buried this time. This was where the purse should be—the notes and pictures, too. It was Emily's own little Time Capsule, something that would symbolize her friendship with *her* Ali forever. Emily's bulletin board looked so bare without all the photos, but she'd have to fill it with new memories. Hopefully, ones that included Aria, Spencer, and Hanna.

"Bye, Ali," Emily said softly. Leaves rustled. A car swished on the street below, its headlights bouncing off the tree trunks. As she was about to leave, she heard another noise. She stopped. It sounded like a snicker.

Emily scanned the trees, but there was no one there. She glanced at the other graves, but nobody moved among the headstones. She even looked up into the sky, as if searching for a blond head among the darkening clouds. She thought about the Web site she'd stumbled upon the other day, a collection of anonymous Twitters from people who'd sworn they'd seen Alison DiLaurentis. *I just saw her walking into J.Crew in Phoenix, AZ,* one of the posts said. *I definitely saw Ali at Starbucks in Boulder,* tweeted another. There were at least fifty of them, new ones being added every day.

"Who's there?" Emily whispered.

Five long seconds passed, but no one answered.

Emily let out a shaky breath. Gathering her strength, she started down the hill to the car. Served her right for hanging around the cemetery at night—all kinds of innocuous sounds and shadows seemed scary in the dark. It was probably just the wind.

Or . . . was it?

THOSE WHO FORGET THE PAST

Imagine it's your senior year and you're sitting in class, less than thrilled to start another day at school. Your spray tan is looking glowing and healthy, and you're wearing your new Juicy hoodie (oh yes, Juicy's on its way back again), and your mind's on your crush, the boy who caddies for your dad at the country club. You're painting your fingernails Chanel Jade, waiting for the teacher to start droning away, when suddenly this new girl walks into the room. She's cute— way cuter than you are—and there's something about her that makes you want to stare and stare. You think, *hmm, maybe she likes green Chanel nail polish, too.* You bet she'd like Golf Caddy boy as well. And you bet if Golf Caddy boy had a choice, he'd choose her over you.

As she looks up and down the aisles, her eyes land on you and stay there. It's like she can see *inside* you, deep down to your wants and desires, the secrets no one knows. You shudder, feeling invaded, but for reasons you can't explain, you also want to tell her your secrets. You want to win her over. You want her to like you best.

"Class," the teacher says, touching the new girl's arm. "This is Laura St. DeLions."

Or *Sara Dillon Tunisi.*

Or *Lanie Lisia Dunstor.*

Or *Daniella Struision.*

Your brain stalls for a moment. There's something familiar about those names, isn't there? Sort of like a scrambled version of your favorite song, or an anagram of a common phrase. The girl looks familiar, too—you've seen that sparkly, I-know-something-you-don't smirk before. You think of a picture on a milk carton you saw long ago. You think of that girl on the news. *Could it be . . . ?*

Nah, you decide. That's crazy. You wave at her and she waves back. Suddenly, you have a feeling she's going to pick you as her brand-new very best friend. You have a feeling your whole life is going to change.

And just like that, it does.

ACKNOWLEDGMENTS

It's with a heavy heart that I write the acknowledgments for the last book in the Pretty Little Liars series. Writing these books has been a thrilling adventure from beginning to end, and I'm still pinching myself that this has been my life for the past four years.

There are many of you who help to make these books what they are, and I can't thank any of you enough. First, Lanie Davis, my day-to-day editor, is always bursting with smart, insightful ideas. Lanie sharpens each book—each chapter and sometimes each sentence!—until it's lean and mean. Sara Shandler, Les Morgenstein, and Josh Bank are all so fully invested in the characters, their stories, and the series as a whole. Kristin Marang creates superb series buzz online—always such a tricky thing! Farrin Jacobs and Kari Sutherland give continued support and fantastic editorial suggestions. And Andy McNicol and Anais Borja at William Morris cheer on the series from start to finish . . .

and send me extra books when I accidentally leave my copy at a bookstore or give it to a rabid reader.

Much love to my parents, Shep and Mindy, who are, at present, obsessed with Wii Fit. Go archery! Hugs to my sister, Alison, who is nothing like the Alison (or Courtney) in these books. Glad we didn't die in the ocean that day! Kisses to my husband, Joel, who was on the phone with me the day I found out that Pretty Little Liars would be a series four years ago. Welcome to Josephine, who has a pinecone tail, and good-bye to Zelda, who sounded like a barge when she paddled in the bay. We will miss you so, so much.

I also want to thank each and every fan of the series. Those of you who pass the books around at school, those of you who make YouTube videos of your ideal PLL cast, those of you who reach out on Facebook and Twitter or share your thoughts on Goodreads, wherever you are, whoever you are, you all have a special place in my heart. And finally, a shout-out to my English teachers at Downingtown Senior High School: the late Mary French, Alice Campbell, and Karen Bald Mapes. You taught me to fear the run-on sentence, you opened my eyes to absurdist drama, bildungsroman novels, and bad Hemingway parodies, and, last but not least, you encouraged me—vehemently, sometimes—to write. You made a huge difference, and I thank you so much.

SUTTON MERCER HAS A LIFE ANY
GIRL WOULD KILL FOR . . . AND
MAYBE SOMEONE DID.

THE
LYING GAME

A DEADLY NEW SERIES FROM

SARA SHEPARD

HARPER TEEN
An Imprint of HarperCollinsPublishers